DATE DUE

C0-DLX-034

© THE BAKER & TAYLOR CO.

PADDY

Also by Kelly P. Gast:

DIL DIES HARD
THE LONG TRAIL NORTH
MURPHY'S TRAIL
MURDER AT MAGPIE FLATS
THE LAST STAGE FROM OPAL

PADDY

KELLY P. GAST

DOUBLEDAY & COMPANY, INC.
GARDEN CITY, NEW YORK
1979

All of the characters in this book are fictitious, and any resemblance to actual persons, living or dead, is purely coincidental.

Library of Congress Cataloging in Publication Data

Gast, Kelly P
Paddy.

I. Title.
PZ4.G2555Pad [PS3557.A847] 813'.5'4
ISBN: 0-385-14291-9
Library of Congress Catalog Card Number 78-18134

Copyright © 1979 by Doubleday & Company, Inc.
All Rights Reserved
Printed in the United States of America
First Edition

PADDY

Chapter 1

Ever since he had butchered the sheep Paddy had been on the run . . . walk, actually, since it's not possible to run any distance with forty pounds of meat and nothing but a raw skin to wrap it in. They had told him there were no Indians in this country and they had lied.

They had said the buffalo were long gone and now he was facing a pair of horns that were—Jesus, Mary, and Joseph, it was nothing but a cow! He was too tired for prayer, too burdened with meat and untanned skins. He had survived Indians, sheepherders, and sheepkillers. Was he to be done in by an outlaw cow? It was enough to weaken a man's faith.

The collie charged like a snarling black cannonball and swung from the cow's muzzle, letting go only when she turned. The brand on her hindquarter looked, to Paddy's limited reading ability, like the £ sign for pounds sterling. The dog attached himself to her hindquarters until the cow's repentance seemed sincere.

When he came back Paddy embraced the collie who, being Scotch, seemed slightly embarrassed. The boy was suddenly so trembly he had to sit. While he waited for strength to return he redid the pack and peeled off the skin he wore. Down here it was turning positively warm. Which caused the meat to ripen rapidly, so that afternoon he camped early and wove drying racks of willow saplings that grew in the creek bottom. He prayed the brisk breeze would dissipate smoke before it could draw any more of those nonexistent Indians. While the meat half dried, half roasted, he explored downstream and found another branch.

Where the creeks joined was a small space where the poplars had been cut down, but for some reason nobody had gone beyond marking out the planned rectangle of a cabin. It was turning dark already—which happened here with a disconcerting suddenness unlike the hours-long gloaming of County Down. He had to call twice before the collie heard him above the noise of the creek. They went back upstream to the fire before coyotes could establish a prior claim. As they came closer the dog's hackles rose.

Paddy was suddenly frightened again. He picked a half-dozen smooth rocks from the creek bottom and crept through the darkness toward his fire. It was not coyotes this time. A huge man lay propped on one elbow before the fire, scoffing down a slice of half-dried, half-roasted, totally unsalted mutton.

Indian? Sure and he was no white man, even if he did wear hat and trousers. The dog growled. Immediately the intruder spun. Paddy was more startled by the flame that shot from the pistol and flared around the cylinder than he was by the noise. By the time he realized he had been shot at again, he also knew the stranger had missed. Paddy's rock did not.

It caught the stranger in the middle of his wide forehead. As he slumped Paddy ran forward and captured the pistol. He was examining it when a fist closed over his ankle.

On his way down he managed to club the barrel of the gun over its owner's head. But it seemed a singularly hard head. The stranger grunted but did not let go. They thrashed for a moment and then Paddy was pinned.

"What the hell the matter with you, boy?" the other man asked. "Don' you know that hurt?"

"And would ye be tellin' me bullets do not?"

The dog whined.

"Well, boy, you can't come sneakin' up on somebody in this country and expect anything better."

"You'd put me in the wrong for savin' what's me own?" The boy studied his assailant. "Ye don't look English. 'Tis little wonder they all kill Indians around here."

The stranger's face turned gradually from puzzlement to amusement. "What you think I am?" he finally asked.

Paddy didn't know. The few Indians he had seen all had straight black hair. This man's was black but there the resemblance ended. There had been a man like this ladling swill when he crossed the sea but Paddy had been too sick for curiosity. In the bustle of transferring from ship to steam cars he had seen a few others. There were none like him in County Down. "If ye're not Indian then why are ye stealin' my meat and tryin' to kill me?"

"Indian?" The stranger laughed. "Boy, I'm an Irishman."

"So's the Pope," Paddy said. "Only he's been so long from home he's clean forgot how to talk Irish."

The stranger removed a hand from Paddy's shoulder and recovered his pistol. "Sit over there on the other side of the fire," he directed. "Oh Jesus!" he added as he dragged himself back the way he had been laying. "You're Irish, ain't you, boy?"

"Me mother always told me I was."

"Well, I'm Irish too. Only difference is I'm a smoked Irishman."

Paddy stared. The tussle with this huge stranger had revived all the half-forgotten aches from his adventures with Indians and sheep.

"Look at my face."

Paddy had been looking at little else. He studied the shiny black skin, the quarter inch of kinky, close knit beard, the grizzling hair like a black sheep on a frosty morning.

"Stay in this country long enough, boy, you gonna look jus' like me."

Paddy didn't know whether to believe him or not. The only effect of unaccustomed sunshine so far had been to grow a fresh crop of freckles and burn the skin off his nose twice a week. Was this black man's face just one big freckle?

"*Guh suira djia Aera!*" he said. When the black man did not respond to an invocation that God free Ireland, Paddy knew he was not Irish. An Orangeman? "And what is it you're doin' here?" he demanded.

The black man's face was abruptly so gray and his eyes so unfocused that Paddy was tempted to dive for the pistol. But before he could make up his mind, intelligence returned to the black eyes across the fire. "They's only one thing a man without a horse's goin' to do in this country."

"Oh? Indians stole mine and I'm makin' no plans to die."

"Indians!" In spite of his pain the black man was amused.

Paddy sighed. Nobody was going to believe him. "Laugh if you will," he growled. "But you'll be dead and all that wool on some savage's tentpole before I'm caught again."

"What makes you think so?"

"'Tis simple. I'm goin' to call me dog now and the two of us are goin' to walk away and leave you rot. And ye'll not do a thing to stop us because if I die you know who will too."

"I'll shoot your dog."

"Do it and I'll clean that hoof so nice it'll take yez a fortnight to die."

"What you know 'bout cleanin' hooves?"

"A damn sight more than I know about doctorin'," the boy said. "But there'll be naught of either till I have that pistol and enough rope to keep yez out of mischief."

The black man stared.

"Or I can just move off into the dark and toss rocks. 'Tis me that's knowin' you'll not be killin' your only chance."

The black man sighed and unloaded the pistol. He tossed it across the fire. When the boy still waited he tossed the cartridges. "They's rope by my saddle." In some obscure way the black man still seemed amused.

"And where might that be?"

"Might be most anywhere but last I saw of it was a hundred yards upstream wrapped round a dead horse."

Paddy stuck the Colt in his belt and hesitated momentarily.

"I'll swear not to hurt you, boy."

"You won't if I can help it," Paddy promised. He caught

up a firebrand and moved off into the darkness. He found the horse and saddle. Moments later he had returned with the rawhide lariat. Still faintly amused, the huge black man submitted to being tied up, which Paddy did very cautiously from behind. Only when the black's arms had been lashed behind him and the remainder of the lariat crisscrossed around his huge torso did Paddy consider the bloody boot. He got out his clasp knife.

"Don't cut it!"

"Boot tonight or foot tomorrow." The boy shrugged. "Or if you'd have it another way, I'll leave yez the pistol with one bullet and then I'll be gone."

The huge man studied him. "You know what you doin'?"

"Maybe not. But I know what has to be done."

There was a moment of silence and then the black man sighed. "Go ahead."

Paddy slit the boot and there was an eruption of pus and blood. After one huge hiss the black man did not move. The boy tossed more wood on the fire and wished for a bucket or a basin. He took a sheepskin to the creek and soaked it. The oily wool was amazingly nonabsorbent but he managed finally to force some water into it. He took it back and wrapped it around the swollen mass of pus and blood. While he was waiting he took the cut-off boot down to the creek and rinsed it clean.

"Boot won't never be no good again."

"I know."

"Then what you do that for?"

The boy put the boot down and began scrubbing at the swollen foot and ankle. He had to take the fleece back to the creek twice before he had loosened enough gore to be able to verify what the boot had hinted. "Thought you had a fall off your horse," the boy muttered.

"I never said that," the black man replied between clenched teeth.

"No saw," the boy said.

The gray face turned even more pallid.

"But I can part the pastern between the bones."

"I ain't no horse!" the black man exploded. "'Sides, you only a boy."

"What day is it?"

"'Bout the start of November, I reckon. Why you ask that?"

"Then I'm sixteen," Paddy said. "Was beginnin' to wonder if I'd ever see my birthday." He picked among the flat stones of the creekbed and began whetting his clasp knife.

"You *sure* you know what you doin'?"

"I'll cut you loose and be on my way," the boy offered.

"Only a boy," the black man mused. "Hit do make a man wonder. Is that why ev'body say 'No Irish need apply'?" His eyes narrowed as he studied the boy's sunburned pink face. "Is it 'cause I'm black? Is that why you don' care if I live or if I die? What is it make you so hard?"

"Might be what I learned in the Old Country," the boy guessed. "And then it might be what I've been learnin' here. 'Twas only a day or two ago a man warned me life was hard; told me I'd no' be long for it if I wouldna' turn hard too. He was a Scotsman. Did you know him?"

"I don' know what you talkin' 'bout, boy."

"You were eatin' his mutton."

The black man shrugged as much as he could with the lariat wrapped around him. "Can't you take this thing off?"

"Don't want you floppin' around if I'm to do any cuttin'."

"Can't you jus' fix it up?"

Paddy finished whetting the knife and passed the blade through the flames, which he had learned was a necessary preliminary to any cutting on a horse. The reasons for this rite were obscure and probably would have been condemned if the priest were ever to learn of them, but since it worked, the men who cared for horses preferred not to discuss trade secrets with outsiders. "If ye've a brain in yer head, ye'll take one look and know what's to be done," the boy said. "Is it yes or am I on me way?"

"Don' understand it," the black man muttered. "How can a boy be so hard?"

"'Tis the way to handle horses," Paddy explained. "Pity the poor beasts and do what you can for them. But always remember they're beasts; their lives are shorter than yours and if you love them overwell they'll break your heart."

"And I'm a horse to you?"

"No."

"Then why you so hard?"

The boy held the cut-off boot before his face and looked at the black man through a three-quarter-inch hole. "Horses kick," he explained. "Horses throw me into the rocks and brambles. But no horse ever shot at me or killed an old man and all his sheep just for the joy of it. And before you go tellin' me it wasn't you, how many guns are there could blow a man's foot near off and tear the belly half out of his horse? And how'd you keep the poor beast movin' this far? No. Don't tell me. I've some feelin' for horses." He brandished the knife. "I'll take your foot off if that's what ye're wantin'. 'Tis more'n ye ivver did for me. But I'll thank you nivver to call me hard again."

The black man glared at Paddy for an instant, then looked away. "Oh," he said.

Paddy felt like saying more but there wasn't that much more to say. Instead, he wondered why he had ever let himself be transported to this accursed country. It wasn't as if he was a criminal.

Chapter 2

He had always been a good boy and done as his mother told him. He had gone to confession regularly and communion as often as any less-than-a-saint. He'd minded his manners and done his work without shirking, and see where it had gotten him!

It had been raining for the better part of the past week. Paddy rode along behind, doing his best not to think. The going was miserable and neither guide nor gentleman felt like conversation. Mr. Bridgeman was a small, leathery man in greasy buckskins who rode a small, almost pony of a horse. He bent low over his horse's neck to miss a low branch.

Less inclined to bend before the elements, Paddy's gentleman pushed the branch aside, letting go just in time to whip water-laden leaves into Paddy's horse's face.

"And him a man says he knows horses!" Paddy muttered to himself. He gripped reins and pommel and braced himself for the explosion, but it did not come. His pony had started to limp over an hour ago and with all this climbing the poor beast was too dispirited to demonstrate his outrage. Paddy patted his neck and made consoling noises. The pony blinked and shook his head as if he shared Paddy's opinion of the man on the middle horse. Blinking and blowing, they plodded through the bracken.

It wasn't really bracken. Somewhere a month ago somebody had explained that the thickets they were encountering at this altitude were service berry—making a great thing out of the way the *e* was pronounced like a broad *ah*—as if it made any difference whether the outlandish fruit were delineated in Romish or Runes. He reached out and picked one of the pale berries. It was as tasteless as everything else in this overrated country.

But then, it had not been Paddy's choice to come here. He studied his gentleman's hacking-coated back and wondered what fascination these mountains could have for any man. There had been talk of a scandal and a hunting expedition until someone became inured to the thought of wife or daughter dishonored—as if honor meant anything to the likes of them—but it was not as if his gentleman had done anything that would necessitate his permanent absence. At least he had assured Paddy's mother that the boy would be home again inside the year.

Paddy tried not to think about such things. Thinking was not exactly illegal, he guessed, but it was not encouraged. On those rare occasions when he had forced himself to trace the convolutions of some idea to its inevitable conclusion Paddy had been neither happier nor more prosperous from what he had learned.

Like right now, for example. The guide had assured them over last night's fire that Indians were a thing of the past in this country. "Been five years since't them savages wiped out Custer—'n good riddance to him," he added with a sly glance over the bottle he held. "But that ol' Medicine Line's two hunnert miles from here and they ain't ary a hostile's dared crost since ol' Sittin' Bull give the Army a huntin' license."

Like right now, Paddy mused. They had been following the tracks of a dozen unshod horses for at least half a day up this so-called trail and neither the guide nor Paddy's gentleman had seen fit to mention it. He wondered if either of the older men had noticed the tracks. And if they had, had either man remarked that these hoofprints were small enough for a nine-hundred-pound Indian pony but sunk as deep in the mud as if they were twelve-hundred-pound Irish hunters? Paddy's mount stumbled and began limping worse. "Uh sorr," he began tentatively.

"Move along now, boy!" his gentleman said in the way gentlemen are wont to give unneeded advice. If Paddy were to urge his string of pack animals any closer, his mount would risk an eyeful of tail.

He made the meaningless sounds used to placate horses and Englishmen, meanwhile keeping his distance. The grizzled, greasy, buckskinned Bridgeman was supposed to be a competent guide. He must have seen those clearly delineated hoofprints in the mud. Paddy guessed there was a simple explanation nobody had bothered to pass on to him.

In this kind of weather, with everything sodden except possibly his gentleman's personal gear, which was enclosed in rubberized sacking, it was just as miserable to camp as to keep slogging on upward into the mountains. Paddy closed his mind to the present, thinking backward on a girl he had known six months ago. He sighed. Nora would be wed and well along to motherhood by now. It wasn't as if there'd been any understanding between them or as if any boy, no matter how handsome and strapping, had any right to make plans.

Padraig Ó Súilleabháin was still days short of sixteen. Anyway, his dalliance had never gotten beyond a kiss or two. If his gentleman had only been capable of a similar restraint around other gentlemen's wives neither of them might have been off with gun and palette in the wilds of America.

"One of those herds of wild—is it cayuses you call them?" Paddy's gentleman had finally taken notice of the tracks.

"Don't rightly know," the guide said. "Ten year ago I'd say it was a war party. But they ain't no Injuns around here."

One of the things about America that amused Paddy was the way the *d* was pronounced as in *individual* or *cordial*. It had taken him a while to realize, however, that Bridgeman's Injuns were not from that subcontinent that Paddy's gentleman called Injuh. "Uh sorr," he tried again, "my horse—"

"Dress up the column!" his gentleman snapped. "Don't string out now."

Paddy shrugged at his gentleman's back and ignored him—letting the beasts string out until they were not kicking mud and jostling one another into spilling loads. There was a pause while his gentleman spread an umbrella and unrolled a map beneath it. Bridgeman gave the map a cursory glance and spat. Paddy had seen the map before. He wondered if the series of marks like the decorations on a sergeant major's sleeve were as meaningless to the bearded Bridgeman as they were to him. While they pondered the map and argued, Paddy dismounted and tried to see to his horse.

"Goddamn it, will you form up and move!"

Paddy mounted and urged the string into motion, feeling no annoyance at his gentleman's peremptory ways. His father, who had once served the Old Gentleman on the Continent, had told Padraig that over there where people spoke tongues even more outlandish than the gentry's, their term for a milord was *goddam*—this being the word that occurred with greatest frequency in the English vocabulary.

Ignoring signs that were obvious even in a pouring rain, his gentleman consulted a hunting-case watch that had been running uncorrected for over a month. Apparently satisfied with what he saw, he touched the crop to his gray. Mr. Bridgeman's glance locked with Paddy's for the briefest of instants and then the man in greasy buckskins was listening to whatever it was the gentleman was saying. Complaining about the scarcity of game, Paddy supposed.

The cañon widened into a meadow that had been sheeped off unless there were some close-grazing animal about here that Paddy had never heard of. They crossed the meadow, squishing fetlock deep, and ahead he saw the hoofprints of horses again overlaying those of sheep.

Between his gentleman and the guide Paddy could see they were going to do it again. Night did not come along with due process in this country the way it did in County

Down, but rather with a disconcerting swiftness that left the unprepared fumbling to make camp in the dark.

"Damn it, Paddy, will you close up now!"

It was against every instinct but Paddy felt he had to speak. There were times when he suspected values were reversed in this unpredictable country—that a man's life was actually deemed more valuable than that of a horse. But Paddy was descended of generations of grooms and it had never been that way in Ireland. "Sorr," he protested, "me harse is gone lame. If I don't look to him now, I'll be afoot in another hour."

His gentleman snarled something unintelligible, which the boy took for permission. He dismounted and made those blowing and whistling noises that horses find comforting. The pony allowed him to inspect its hoof. The flint was sharp as a piece of broken bottle and driven deep into the frog. Paddy worried at it with the tip of his clasp knife and finally got it free. Blood came out with it.

Still the rain came down with a persistent steadiness that reminded him of home, though there seemed a promise of something harder here than in the gentle welcoming rains of County Down. Guide and gentleman had disappeared noiselessly into the susurration of raindrops, but the boy knew he could follow the trail of their shod beasts easily among all those untrimmed hooves. He searched the pannier of the nearest pack animal until he found a whiskey bottle smeary with pungent pine tar. By the time he had finished stuffing a bit of tarred rag into the wounded frog of his pony it was suddenly turning dark.

He mounted again and the beast was willing but he had hurt it getting that flint out. To slog along through water and mud would do the poor brute more damage if he were not to give that pine tar time to cauterize and clot the wound. Paddy stared into the growing darkness where his gentleman and the guide had disappeared. They couldn't be more than a mile or so ahead but already he could hardly see the ground.

Devil take them! His gentleman would be somewhat more ill-tempered than usual come morning, but it would be good for his High Church soul to spend a night without full kit and folding rubber bathtub. Hadn't he come to America to rough it? Paddy knew he could find them if he were willing to abuse the horse. Also knew the pair of them would chivvy him into doing the lion's share of the work setting up camp. Still . . .

He had just about decided to walk it and let the pony hop along on three legs when he heard a shot. Paddy said something that sounded like *"Noch gurruch shin farrug err naeev,"* but that is spelled in a totally unrecognizable manner and that, seven thousand miles away, is taken to mean, "Wouldn't that anger a saint?" The shot meant either guide or gentleman had shot something for supper and it would be up to Paddy to skin it.

He was standing beside his lame pony when suddenly there was a popping fusillade like galloglasses at the butts. This time the shots seemed closer. There was the whine of a ball glancing off rock and one of the packhorses screamed. Then the whole string was galloping off into the darkness, leaving Paddy to stand beside his lame pony. There was another shrill scream and it took him an instant to realize it was not a horse that had made that noise.

Hooves thundered and a pony came rocketing out of the darkness. The hatless rider snatched the reins of Paddy's lame mount and gave the boy a slap across the ear and before he knew it the boy was standing alone in the wet darkness with naught but his clothes and his clasp knife. It had all happened so swiftly he didn't quite believe it.

He squinted into the darkness and wished the rain would let up long enough to see which way he was going. It didn't, so he walked blindly until he felt the brush. He burrowed in until he hoped nobody would be able to find him, then settled down to wait for his gentleman to come back and make the sort of remarks that might be expected to a boy who had just managed to lose his gentleman's kit and his whole string of horses.

Even in this unpredictable country, to be boxed on the ears by a horse-stealing stranger was not Paddy's normal way of ending the day. But if his gentleman saw fit to lead him where brigands abound, then it was up to Himself to assess the consequences. Still, Paddy knew what shots and screams in the night could lead to in County Down. He worried.

But groom, son of a groom, son of an Irish climate, and still short of his sixteenth birthday, Padraig Ó Súilleabháin discovered some hours later that he had slept and meanwhile the rain had finally stopped.

He moved cautiously, scooting through the brush until he could see the meadow again. Rain had blurred the edges of the tracks but it still looked like the same hoofprints they had followed all day yesterday—prints of small, nine-hundred-pound ponies driven as deep into the ground as if they were twelve-hundred-pound Irish hunters. Either these horses were carrying fourteen-stone riders or . . .

So where now was his gentleman? For a moment Paddy was tempted to shout, but that didn't seem wise. He stood at the edge of the meadow trying to see past the rising sun and struggling to wring water from his clammy tweeds. Neither project was wholly successful.

There is something about fifteen years, eleven months, and three weeks that renders man especially vulnerable to an empty stomach. Paddy walked the edge of the meadow, skirting the brush, filling his mouth with service berries, and wondering if their vaunted taste belonged to some other month of the brief mountain summer. His stomach was churning from the acid fruit.

Also, he knew that by now his gentleman should have been turning the mountain air blue with his goddamns, pouring the frustrations of a night without comforts onto the boy who was to blame for it all.

He walked toward where guide and gentleman had disappeared, praying they would have done their own skinning and butchering by now. He was perfectly willing to listen to his gentleman blame it all on Paddy—as if the boy hadn't tried to ask about all those tracks and what that many mounted horses could mean way up here where there was supposed to be nobody.

But bedamned if he wasn't going to give Himself a piece of his mind if his gentleman couldn't at least offer a slice of cold meat before he began inventorying Paddy's sins. 'Twasn't as if Paddy or his mother owed this one any favors like it was with the Old Gentleman (and may God see that he gets a cool corner in hell). But the young gentleman . . . if he wanted to go whorin' about with other men's wives 'twas only proper that he spend a few damp nights on this earth unless he'd rather spend seven thousand hot ones in Purgatory.

The service berries were reacting violently in Paddy's empty stomach and he resolved that this time, no matter how Mr. Bridgeman might gang up against him and side with the man who paid his wages—this time Paddy wasn't going to be bawled out for something that was not his fault. And if his gentleman didn't like it he could go find himself a new groom.

He was well out of the meadow now and the trail was narrow. He studied the muddle of tracks in the growing light and picked out the shod hooves of the guide's and his gentleman's mounts. Paddy followed the tracks through another tiny meadow where the cañon widened and the creek's roar came down to a conversational level. He gasped on another half mile, climbing steadily until trees were squat and gnarly, all streaming out in the same direction like the smoke from cottage chimneys.

It was up where the grass was scanty and the ground cover mostly moss and velvety leaved things like grow on the north sides of rock walls in Ireland that Paddy finally found Mr. Bridgeman and his gentleman. He stared, wondering how a horse could have done all that damage. But even as he stared, Paddy knew it was not horses that had done this to the battered and bloody bodies that lay beside the trail.

Suddenly service berries on an empty stomach were too much. He turned his head and retched, knowing that in some evasive boyish way he had been expecting this all along and yet not willing to believe it would really happen. But when he turned back wet-eyed and weak Mr. Bridgeman and his gentleman were still there—still bloody. Still.

A moment ago Paddy had been ready to tell his gentleman to go pack it in. Now he remembered how long since they had last seen a town—how long since Ireland. He forced himself to look down on his gentleman's bloody bald head and found himself relenting. If God saw fit to provide a cool corner in hell, he hoped his gentleman might have a chance at it. Mr. Bridgeman too.

Chapter 3

Somewhere in the back of Paddy's mind was a feeling that if he could just make himself wake up all this would turn out never to have happened, that he might still be back in County Down and about ready to sit down to a steaming dish of stelk.

But every time he opened his eyes he was still here, still wet and hungry, and his gentleman was dead. Finally the boy gave up and went down to the creek, which was noticeably smaller at this height. He began whittling at the straightest of the gnarled saplings.

It took several eternities to hack through the tough, timberline growth with his clasp knife and when he finally had a stick free Paddy discovered it might take even longer to dig enough hole to foil the animals that were sure to follow him. He jumped down into the creek and waded its narrow course until he had found an undercut bank a couple of feet above the present water level.

He got Mr. Bridgeman's bloodless, mutilated body under the overhang, struggling mightily against rigor mortis. He was dragging his gentleman down to join Mr. Bridgeman when he realized abruptly how utterly soaked and miserable he was, and simultaneously that his gentleman no longer needed so fancy a coat.

Paddy sat on the creekbank for several minutes thinking. Something—perhaps that thing the priests kept calling a conscience—kept telling him he shouldn't. But common sense told the boy if he didn't get some warm clothes to replace the blankets that had departed along with everything else . . .

"I wouldn't take it, sorr, if I didn't need it worse than you," he muttered as he struggled to get the hacking coat and waistcoat from his gentleman's rigid remains. He thought for a moment about boots and socks but, having experimented with Himself's castoffs before, Paddy knew they would be too small.

Still not feeling right about it, he levered his gentleman in beside Mr. Bridgeman, whose greasy buckskins would have remained inviolate even if he had not been such a small man. The boy climbed atop the cut bank to dig and pry until the earth collapsed. When he was sure they were completely covered, Paddy knelt to say a prayer for their poor damned Protestant souls.

So now what? As long as he could keep busy the boy had managed to postpone the unrewarding business of thinking. The wet hacking coat was a trifle narrow for his less-than-sixteen-year-old shoulders. Its tight-pinched waist and flaring skirts could never be forced around him. He put it over him like a cape but even with his gentleman's waistcoat under his own sodden tweeds the boy felt a chill misery that not even the watery sun could alleviate. And the worst thing about it was that Paddy could not honestly say whether he mourned most for his gentleman or for the breakfast he had expected after a night in the wild without supper.

He struggled to recall talk around the campfire, wishing he had not been so nearly asleep as soon as he finished evening chores. They had often argued over the better route through these mountains, his gentleman offering a map and Mr. Bridgeman insisting, "Just because it's on a piece of paper don't necessarily make it so." Their single point of agreement was that once over the summit it would be only a couple of days' ride into Fort Rudge.

But two days' ride could turn into three or four days' walk —if his boots held out. And he was hungry already. He fingered the sharpened stick and thought momentarily of making a cross. But he might need it. He gave the collapsed creekbank a final glance. "And may God show yez more kindness than ivver ye showed me," he muttered as he began walking.

The first couple of miles were uphill until there were no more trees and the ground was bare and rocky as the sea-facing links of home. The creek became a trickle and then nothing. Paddy was breathing with difficulty and, never having been this high before, thought he was dying of hunger. Then trees reappeared and gradually he felt more alive. But he didn't understand what had happened until he noticed that the reborn creek now flowed in the opposite direction.

By noon the trees were still sparse but no longer gnarly, as they had been up near the summit. Paddy paused to pull off still-wet boots and socks. He stretched flat in the sunshine. The griping emptiness of his stomach had settled into that dull, chronic complaint that was part of the business of being Irish.

Not that Paddy had personally suffered all that much during the great hungers. His people had lived in relative comfort on the Old Gentleman's estate. But they had lived under the Angle eye of a steward who saw that all surplus went to the hogs and not to starving Irish neighbors. And for this Paddy's family had transmuted guilt into an undifferentiating hatred of all things English.

But it was this relative comfort that had made Paddy a head taller than his runted, chronically starved peers, given him shoulders broader and feet bigger than his gentleman's, though the boy was still not finished growing. He ran a hand through bright red hair, felt his chin for the beginnings of beard, and picked until he had peeled another layer of dead skin from the tomato-colored, totally untannable protuberance in the middle of his long-lipped face.

He had to get back to County Down, which would mean letters he didn't know how to write, to heirs he didn't know. Facing a rapidly blueing sky, he tried not to think about it.

A bird flew over. Moments later he saw another. They were large black birds with separate pinion feathers like ravens. Then as he focused attention Paddy saw they were what Mr. Bridgeman had called buzzards. His first thought was that he hadn't done a proper job of covering up the grave. Then he saw the buzzards were circling somewhere downhill ahead of him. A third scavenger joined the circle. Paddy pulled his half-dried socks on and laced his boots. He picked up the sharpened stick and began walking. Soon there was grass again, tiny new shoots coming up through the drying remains of summer. But the old grass had all been cropped off short. He squinted, trying to deduce the focal point of the birds' orbiting. Then he heard the growl. He had not seen a dog since the last time he had seen a house. Paddy gripped the sharpened stick and stepped off the trail.

It was a bitch coyote with two half-grown pups. When she saw Paddy the bitch gave a single yip and the trio streaked off into the timber. He went up to see what they had been tearing apart. It was a black lamb.

Given time, the coyotes would have left nothing but skin and bones for the buzzards. But, being gourmets, they had fed first on the vital organs, leaving one hindquarter barely touched. Paddy glanced skyward past the buzzards and said, "Bless us, O Lord, and these thy gifts, which of thy bounty we are about to receive through Christ, Our Lord. Amen."

He whetted his clasp knife on a rock and began skinning out the ham. He was so hungry he had to spit constantly lest his mouth run over. He laid the meat carefully atop the fresh skin.

After a fortnight of rain there was no such thing as dry wood. He pried at fallen logs, hoping for some tiny unsaturated spot on their undersides. Finally he had gathered a hatful of twigs of doubtful combustibility. He banged a fallen limb repeatedly over a rock, sending numbing tingles up to his shoulder blades before the wood parted to reveal dry punk. Still salivating like the Scotch giant, he hunted for flint

—any stone that would strike a spark. The buzzards gave up and flew away, heading south.

It had been difficult for the last fortnight to start a fire even with the aid of the matches Himself had furnished—great yellow-headed things that cracked like pistol shots, then sputtered endlessly before bursting into a flame that water-soaked wood ignored. He went to the opposite side of the clearing, hoping the rain might not have driven so penetratingly there.

And finally, beneath a windfall, he found a hatful of dry leaves inside a packrat's nest. Ready to cook, he returned to pick up his leg of lamb. It was gone.

For an instant Paddy thought he had lost his mind or that he was dreaming again. Then he saw the black wooled skin where he had left it. On the skyline he also saw the coyote bitch with something in her long-pointed jaws. She gave him a final backward glance and disappeared over the ridge. The empty-mouthed pups lingered to look at him. To Paddy it seemed as if they were laughing.

It was a terrible temptation to fling his hard-bought kindling, kick, scream, call down God's wrath upon this accursed land. But he was too hungry to waste all that energy. There was still some left if he could control his squeamishness over eating coyote leftovers.

He clanged the back of his knife blade against a rock, skinning knuckles until finally the rotten wood smoldered. Several puffing minutes later he had a small fire. He cut and trimmed, hunting out bits of relatively untouched meat. He had to sharpen his knife again before he could trim these gobbets into strips to wind around his stick.

The fire was blazing enough to take large pieces of wet wood now, sending a great plume of grayish-black smoke straight up into the clear afternoon sky.

All that smoke made Paddy uneasy but there was not enough dry wood in this entire territory for him to do anything about it. He held his stick over the fire and after the first rank whiff the meat began to smell positively appetizing. He had scorched it nearly to edibility when increasing uneasiness made him glance up. A man on horseback was looking at him from across the meadow.

He was hatless and even from this distance Paddy saw from the way he sat the horse that the man was riding English style. It wasn't until the stranger turned slightly that Paddy saw the braids and understood. The bareback Indian urged his pony to a trot.

So this was how it was to end. Paddy discovered that he was not really afraid to die. He just hoped it would be over quickly. He began saying an Act of Contrition.

The Indian, who knew a death song when he heard one, watched with the detached interest of an anthropologist. But Paddy's ritual came to a premature end as he smelled meat scorching. He snatched the spit from the fire, and the Indian's detachment departed along with Paddy's stick, which the Indian sent flying with a flick of his feather-bedecked lance.

They studied one another, Paddy kneeling at his fire and the Indian sitting his horse, his lance point on target. His face was not painted but its symmetry was ruined by a lumpy swelling, as if he had bad teeth in his lower jaw. The Indian studied Paddy and frowned. With the lance tucked beneath his elbow he muttered and made an ear-boxing gesture.

Paddy could not understand the other's discomfiture when the Indian discovered he had counted coup on a boy still too young to grow a beard. But with the ear-boxing gesture Paddy abruptly knew this was the man who had knocked him down and run off his string of horses. This had to be one of the lot who had killed his gentleman and Mr. Bridgeman.

A moment ago he had been saying an Act of Contrition. Now as fury boiled through him Paddy knew he was going to die unshriven and unrepentant. He caught a firebrand and hurled it at the Indian's face. Neither Indian nor horse flinched. The lance point touched Paddy's throat.

The boy braced himself, damned if he would say another word of prayer for an unearned death. The point of the lance moved away from his throat. The horse backed off and the Indian gestured. Paddy learned that his end was not to be that easy.

Any other day of his life Paddy might have consented to being a moving target. But within the past twenty-four hours he had lost kit and horses, had buried his gentleman, and had just had the same trick played on him that he had played on the coyotes. Paddy had been raised to believe that only the English could act with such total disregard of the common decencies. He glared at his tormentor across the gulf of no common language and wished for words to express his rage.

The Indian prodded.

"I'll not run!" Paddy snarled. But under the lance's prodding he had to walk. He allowed the Indian to herd him across the meadow. Each time the man on horseback tried to coax him into a run the boy turned and stood to face him, glaring and waiting. The Indian seemed amused.

He kept it up for the better part of a mile, driving the boy back up the path he had followed down from the timberline. As Paddy walked slowly, bleeding from half a dozen efforts to hurry him on, he tried to guess what was planned for him. By now the Indian must know there would be no sport trying to run down a man on foot. If he wanted to kill him Paddy would long ago have gone the way of his gentleman and Mr. Bridgeman.

Finally the boy stumbled once more and could not get up. This time the lance did not prod. The Indian's lumpy face was expressionless. Pointing uphill, back the way Paddy had come from, he said, "Boy, you go." He pointed back downhill with his lance and added, "Boy, you die." The Indian turned and trotted his pony off down the trail, leaving the boy a day hungrier, with a day's less shoe leather. It was late afternoon.

Chapter 4

Suddenly Paddy realized that he was not going to die. Not immediately, anyway. His clothes had pretty well dried out by now, and in addition to his own tweeds, he still wore his gentleman's waistcoat and hacking coat. A night on the timberline promised to be no worse than the last rain-soaked eternity he had shivered through up here. But how long could he live without food?

Quite a while, he supposed, if those stories about the great hunger were true. But sooner or later a man's stomach would rebel against grass. The real question was, how long could he keep moving? He remembered how many days it had taken to reach this point on well-fed horses. He knew perfectly well that even with new socks and boots he was never going to walk it back.

Still, he stumped onward until he was once more where he had buried his gentleman and Mr. Bridgeman. Would he ever be free of them? As he looked at the collapsed creekbank he remembered whispered accounts of terrible deeds during the great hunger. He hurried past their graves, struggling to make the most of the dying light.

There had to be white men somewhere nearby. He remembered the grazed-off meadow, the lamb he had almost eaten. Red-skinned savages didn't raise sheep. Why couldn't he have paid more attention to Mr. Bridgeman's descriptions of this country?

The creek noise here was still too loud for him to hear anything else. He wanted to move on but he was stumbling in the darkness. He decided there weren't too many more things could happen to him. He burrowed into the brush at the edge of the trail and tried to sleep.

But sleep did not come immediately. Instead, he wondered what it was that the Indian was protecting beyond where he had buried his gentleman. Belatedly, the boy realized the savage had not really intended to kill him. He had merely wanted to make sure the boy did not move any farther in that direction. Why? And then Paddy finally did fall asleep, only to be immediately plagued with dreams of stelk: minor mountains of cabbage and potato mash surrounded by palisades of crisp bacon. He dreamed of praties with buttermilk, of herring in all its many-boned splendor. His vision of mutton was so vivid he could actually hear that animal's plaint against the world's injustice.

Then Paddy was awake and studying a skyful of ragged, fast-moving clouds. He shivered. The sun was not up yet but there was light to see the meadow—empty as it had been last night. But he heard the sound again. Paddy was not familiar with the kinds of sheep they raised in this country, save that they seemed to have finer wool than the baritone-voiced beasts of his home island. He had discovered that several American deer and antelope made similar sounds. He also knew that in the Ould Sod he could be hanged for what was passing through his mind.

The single baa was so near the edge of his hearing that he was still unsure whether his imagination was not playing some trick with the murmur of the creek. From a hundred feet up the hillside he could see better but up there he could no longer hear the lamb. "You're wishin' it all," he told himself. And then finally he heard a dog barking. Somewhat later he had pushed his way over a ridge and down into another meadow where sheep grazed. The black border collies raised such a fuss that it was the herder who found Paddy. "Stand quiet and don't move your hands," was his greeting.

It was the largest opening the boy had ever seen in a gun barrel. "'Twould seem there's damn little to choose between an English speaker and any other savage," he said.

"My God, an Irishman!" the herder said disgustedly. He lowered his rifle and waited for the boy to come closer. He was a grizzling man with a face as craggy as the pastures of Roscommon. They stared at each other for a moment and then the old man spoke in a language as lacking in verbs as is the country in every other amenity. Literally, he asked, "And would self be having the Saxon?"

Paddy struggled with Highland Gaelic, which was close enough to understand but not near enough to the Irish for easy converse. "I have the devil's tongue," he said.

"So what are you doin' this far from home?"

"Starving."

"Ye could ha' done that in Ireland."

Paddy told him what had happened.

"Indians! Lad, ye're daft. Save for those poor creatures under the guns of the fort there's no savage alive in all this territory."

"Then was it the Little People killed my gentleman and stole my horses—and poked all these holes in me wi' their fairy wands?"

"Did they wear hats?"

Paddy stared for a moment. "Only one I got a good look at had his hair braided. Had a feather in it."

"Only one?"

"One man, one feather."

The Scotsman shook his head and led Paddy back to his camp, which consisted of a tent of weathered canvas floored with the hides of winter-killed sheep. Before the tent a small fire still warmed the hemispherical iron pot that hung from a green sapling tripod. Paddy devoured several bowls of a mutton and barley stew flavored with the wildest and most pungent onions he had ever tasted.

"You're sure it was an Indian?" the herder persisted when Paddy had finally put aside the bowl.

"He had a face like a gargoyle; hair like a horse's tail, and he rode without any of those odd bits of wood and leather the people in this country keep callin' saddles."

"Oh you know about those things?"

"We have horses in County Down."

The herder glanced at Paddy's near-gone boots. "Cows too, I suppose."

"And don't they have them in this country?"

"Oh aye, they have them here all right."

Paddy was puzzled at the herder's foreboding air. He had several other questions, but it was warm inside the tent and his stomach was full.

Toward nightfall he awakened long enough to scoff down another bowl of stew. Next day he helped the old man strike the tent and load it along with everything else onto a pair of beasts rather like the donkeys Paddy knew from home, save that these were considerably smaller. "Where are we going?" he asked.

"Downhill," the old man said with a glance at scudding clouds. "Ahead of the snow."

"Will there be Indians?"

"Och lad, 'tis no Indians I'm afeard of."

They moved several miles slantwise of the trail Paddy had followed up into this country—crossing a hogback ridge and descending a couple of thousand feet. Even here the grass was scant and the herd scattered in search of it. The old man and his dogs went out to round them up for the evening, leaving Paddy to set up camp and refill the pot.

Paddy wondered how long it would take before the old man and the sheep would be close enough to civilization for him to find a constable and free himself of what had happened to his gentleman and Mr. Bridgeman. The camp was close to another small creek and its noise competed with the constant blather of sheep. Overhead buzzards circled awaiting their share, which would come after the coyotes ringing the camp had extracted their tribute from overworked dogs. Paddy was blowing and fanning, struggling to coax a blaze from the cooking fire when he heard a shot.

He was stampeding for the brush when he remembered that the old man had befriended him, treated him with more humanity than he had ever gotten from his gentlemen. He checked himself and listened, trying to figure from which direction the shot had come. But the echoes were too confusing. Maybe a dog would come to tell him something was wrong. He waited but there was neither dog nor any more shots. He was resigning himself to a time-wasting square search when he saw the old man heading back for camp with a small antelope over his shoulders.

"Do you like it better than mutton?" the boy asked as he floured slices of liver and dropped them into a soot-encrusted skillet.

"'Twould take more teeth than I've got to tell the difference," the herder said. "But the man who owns these sheep sleeps better when I'm not eatin' up his profit and these poor sleekit beasties're not eatin' up his grass." He busied himself with cleaning his venerable weapon.

Paddy studied the old man's gun, plagued with a feeling that he had seen it before.

"Nae doot," the old man said. "Every castle in the Old Country's a hundred o' them fanned over the library walls. Sin' the Army quit usin' the old Brown Bess they're cheaper than wallpaper."

Then Paddy remembered them from his rare incursions into his gentleman's great house. But this Tower musket had had a foot of barrel sawed off and the flint lock reworked to take a cap.

"Did you bring it from the Old Country?" the boy asked.

"Only one in the territory," the old man said. "Maybe in the whole damned savage continent." He finished ramming home a ball, jammed a cap into the nipple, and eased the massive hammer back down to a half cock.

"How far will it shoot?"

The old man regarded him with some amusement. "Forever, if it's all downhill," he said. "But if you're countin' on hittin' somethin', I wouldna try over a hundred yards."

Then, remembering how close to the bone his own young

life had been, the old man came as close to smiling as is possible for a Highlander. "Would ye like to try it?"

Paddy would like nothing better. He knew horses but in spite of his gentleman and Mr. Bridgeman both carrying rifles, the boy had never fired one.

"That ball is three quarters of an inch across," the old man warned. "Hold it tight to the shoulder or ye'll ache for a fortnight." He went on to explain things like sights and how high above the target one must aim at various distances. Paddy gave the skillet a quick check and then took aim in the dying light, standing to point the musket at the white patch of a lightning-blasted pine.

With a foot sawed off the barrel it was not so hard to balance as the boy had been expecting. He struggled to remember the old man's instructions and yet knew when the trigger snapped that he had jerked it instead of squeezing. For the tiniest of instants he thought the gun had misfired. Then smoke and flame erupted from the barrel and Paddy was abruptly sitting, still holding the gun in a firm, two-fisted grip.

"That's no' bad for a start," the old man said. "Tomorrow when there's light ye can try it again."

"Did I hit it?"

"Almost." The old man managed not to smile.

As he scoffed down his share of antelope liver Paddy became gradually aware that his right shoulder was aching even worse than all the scrapes and punctures he had endured from the lumpy-jawed Indian. They portioned out the remains of the liver to the dogs, and the old man gave the herd a final lookover before turning in. In the morning they moved again, setting up camp some three miles and another thousand feet downhill. And Paddy learned how much powder to pour into the weapon, how to cut a patch and ram home a ball.

The mountains were less vertical here, and below camp the boy saw several miles of gradually descending tableland. Down below, the grass seemed considerably greener than up here among the rocks and cañons. He wondered why they did not move farther, but the old man volunteered no information. Nor would he let Paddy fire the musket in their new location.

"Why not?" the boy asked.

The Scotsman glanced at the grazing merinos. "'Tis no' easy to lay low wi' all that pother," he sighed, "but I think it best to make no noise."

"Indians?"

"No, lad. No Indians here. But there's grass and there's cattle." Then, seeing the boy's uncomprehending stare, the old man went on to explain. "This, lad, is the Great American Desert. Looks green and it looks big but there's a three-way tug-of-war agoin' on among antelope, sheep, and cows. Now ye'd think there's room for all—that is, ye'd think so if ye were no' a cattleman or an Indian or a buffalo or some-such unprofitable creation of Our Lord.

"In this year of eighteen and eighty-one there are no more buffalo. And any Indian's lang syne had his horns sawed off. So now all that remains for King Cattleman to do is get the sheep out and see that the plow never gets in." The old man paused to stoke a pipe. "Ye'll forgi' me, lad, but I've no great love for sheep meself, though my reasons be summat different from the cattlemen of these parts."

Paddy supposed he was to ask a question at this point but he didn't know what to ask.

"D'ye know where Roscommon is, lad?"

Paddy didn't.

"'Tis less than two hundred miles north o' your own County Down—wi' a bit o' water in between. They tell me there're people astarvin' in Ireland these days. 'Tis no' true in the Highlands."

"People don't starve in Roscommon?"

"They do not, lad. Ye can walk for miles and see the stonework and chimneys of unroofed cottages and ye'll never once see a bairn goin' hungry. Ye'll never see one damned soul since they moved all the people out to make room for the sheep."

"They?"

"Aye, They," the old man growled. "But ye must na think 'tis because they hate the Scots and the Irish. They've done just as well starvin' out the smallholders in England wi' their Removal Acts. 'Tis to feed their damned machines in Manchester that they'd turn out a man's been three hundred years on the land and replace him wi' a sheep." He sighed and dedicated himself to his pipe for a moment.

"But now I'm bankin' near six pound a month tendin' them same blameless beasts as overran me father's corn and pulled down his fences and sent Himself off to starve. 'Tis a cruel world, lad. If ye dinna' learn that ye're no' long for it."

And Paddy had thought life hard in County Down. He stared into the darkness thinking about six pounds a month in a safe place. Then he remembered an Indian lance poking his back.

"So what're you goin' t' do wi' your young life?" the old man asked. "Ye'll no' be goin' home again an' gi' your mother another mouth to feed?"

Paddy hadn't thought of it this way before. Now he saw that without his gentleman, life in County Down would never be the well-nourished, paddock-bounded existence he had always known.

"Ye can ha' my job if ye want it."

Paddy stared, not all that enthusiastic at the prospect of spending the rest of his life with sheep.

"Ye can ha' the whole damned kit and camp," the old man added gloomily. "I've had me share o' this country. Course," he added, "ye'd be a fool to take it without knowin' what ye're in for."

"Indians?"

"Damn it, lad, there're no Indians here."

"D'ye think I killed my gentleman and Mr. Bridgeman?"

the boy flared. "D'ye think I stole all the horses and kit and poked a half-dozen holes in me own back?"

"Aye. I'd forgotten that. 'Tis enough to make a man ponder."

The old Scotsman was still pondering when the shooting started.

Chapter 5

It was outrageous. Every time Paddy reached some turning point and was ready to make a decision something else had to come along and take it out of his hands. Would life ever treat him like an equal—or would he always be a stableboy? Then as the shooting increased until it was pouring into the camp from three sides, he realized there were worse prospects in sight than living as a groom. War whoops, howls, and bullets poured into the camp.

If only he had a rifle. But the old man snatched it up as the first round scattered the campfire. "Run, lad!" he shouted. "Save yourself."

Paddy did not hang around for detailed instructions. He stampeded away from the firelight, heading blindly in the only direction from which no shots came.

The dogs were struggling to preserve order, but every sheep seemed to have the same idea as Paddy. He found himself in the middle of the herd, rebounding blindly from woolly masses, being trampled by tiny hooves as sharp as the Indian's lance. He struggled to his feet and was once more running blindly into the darkness, no longer intent on escaping the shooting. Now he would settle for just being able to extricate himself from this mass of sheep.

Suddenly he was—not exactly falling, but he was running and sliding much faster than he had planned. And so were the sheep. In this ravine the sound of their blather was so all encompassing that he could no longer even hear the whooping and shooting. He pitched forward and fell on top of a mass of kicking, squirming animals. And like a waterfall, the rest of them came cascading down the slope to land on top of him. To Paddy it seemed as if every sixty pounds of sheep strove to drive four spikes into his back, his buttocks, his head, and his shoulders. If he were to turn his head to look up, these indiscriminate gougers would have his eyes. If he stayed face down, one of those razor-sharp hooves could sever his spinal cord. Face buried in stinking wool, he struggled to breathe.

Then as sheep continued piling nonstop atop him the boy faced a new problem. Those beneath him were no longer struggling. If he didn't claw up out of this death pit soon . . . With the prospect of imminent death to focus his attention, the boy found strength to burrow his way upward through more active layers of sheep until he was once more breathing—and once more being stabbed by the hooves of the latest arrivals.

How long could it go on? He struggled up and was knocked down again. But by now the sheep had nearly filled the small ravine. Clouds parted for a moment and he recognized the Big Dipper. If he headed toward it he would be moving away from camp—he thought. He clawed and crawled across an ocean of dying sheep until finally he was on bare ground again. He kept on crawling, feeling his careful way lest he fall into another whirlpool of flesh and wool.

But none of the sheep had gotten across the first cañon. He was on bare ground now, just beginning to realize how much worse he was going to be hurting before long. He kept moving toward the Big Dipper, listening for shots as he moved away from the nightmare racketing of dying sheep. He wondered if the old Scotsman had survived. But mostly he wondered if he would live through the night. Jesus, Mary, and Joseph! He hadn't hurt this bad since a lovesick mare had planted a hoof on his shoulder. But this time the ache was all over his body!

He struggled to keep moving toward the Big Dipper— away from the hellish racket behind him. But the stars were wheeling crazily now. And then he couldn't see the stars at all.

Dawn brought an abrupt awakening. He was so cold he couldn't even shiver, but when he tried to move, Paddy learned that last night's pain had only been a prelude. His wrists and ankles were as black and blue as his shoulder that time the mare had confused him with a different kind of stud.

Sweat spurted, and then he was shivering uncontrollably. He forced himself onto hands and knees and tried to guess where he was. Couldn't be more than half a mile from camp. But which way? He listened. Surely they couldn't have killed every sheep.

The effort not to howl every time he moved brought blood to his numb limbs and then the pain was worse. Still, he discovered that he could stand. He recognized landmarks and knew which way camp was. As he topped the ridge scattered handfuls of sheep still grazed.

The sun had still to rise and he was suddenly shivering again—this time so badly he fell to his knees. Ahead was a ravine filled with dead sheep. If he didn't get warm soon— get out of this chilling wind . . . He burrowed into the top layer of dead animals and shivered himself almost to sleep, wondering if it was his imagination that sent a tremor through his bed. Then he realized some of those poor brutes down below must still be alive! He struggled to pull dead animals off the top but he ran out of strength. The movement ceased and he fell into something between a faint and a sleep.

The next time he woke he was warm and not in such mortal agony. He rolled up a pants leg and studied his black-and-blue shin. This was the way he would look if someone were to go over his body systematically with a hammer. But he could move. He struggled up out of the ravine.

There was neither shepherd nor body where the tent had been shagged into the campfire. The cast-iron pot was shattered. Even the pulled skins that had lined the floor of the tent had been pitched into the fire and scorched into stinking uselessness. One of the collies appeared abruptly and poked his nose in Paddy's face.

"Where is he?" the boy demanded. "Where's your master?"

It was not idle foolishness on the boy's part. He had watched these dogs follow the old Scotsman's shouted instructions from half a mile away and he was convinced a border collie was fully as smart, possibly even more intelligent, than the gentleman Paddy had just buried.

"Where's the shepherd?" he repeated. The dog licked Paddy's hand and whined. The boy sighed. If the old man were alive, in need of help, the dog would be doing everything under the sun to lead or drag Paddy to him. But the dog had already transferred his allegiance to Paddy.

The boy thought a moment. Even before the raid there had been no shovel in camp. And if the old man's body were anywhere in sight, the collie would be grabbing his sleeve and leading him there. Paddy had enough problems without looking for a body that was either buried beneath a thousand sheep or so far away he would never find him. He had a dog now but, apart from that, the boy was alone again.

He tried to remember the Scotsman's name for this dog and couldn't. The collie drove his nose into Paddy's hand again and made a growling, snuffling sound. "You'll be Dorrga," the boy decided, which, in Irish, means *gruff*. If the dog disapproved he did not say so.

The Scotsman had been a Protestant and therefore a heathen. But the old shepherd had hated the English. Paddy knelt to say a prayer for a man whose soul could not be all bad.

When he was finished the boy struggled to his feet and studied the scattered herd. The dogs had all disappeared but one. Both donkeys were gone. There was no hint of the Scotsman, nor of his ancient weapon. Was he buried under ten layers of sheep, the way Paddy had almost ended up? Or was he out somewhere beneath a vortex of buzzards? There were so many of them in the sky that it would be impossible to look for him. Perhaps the old man had managed to get clean away.

And who had done all this? Was it the same lot had done in his gentleman and Mr. Bridgeman? Indians? Bridgeman had insisted there were no more Indians in this country. And Mr. Bridgeman had ended up scalped. The old Scotsman had also been positive there were no savages here. Civilized men would not do this. Civilized men would kill other men. But civilized men would not destroy sheep which, even in this benighted wilderness, must be worth at least four shillings apiece. It would be like setting fire to a packet of pound notes.

Paddy couldn't figure it out. Indians had killed his gentleman and Mr. Bridgeman. They had also stolen the full kit and every horse in the string. Was there anything in this camp worth stealing? Worth killing for? If there was, it was no longer here. He studied the sky and remembered the old man had been moving down ahead of the snow.

The boy studied his ragged tweeds and nearly done-in boots. He thought guiltily about the sheep. Quite apart from their monetary value, they were God's creatures, and few of them would survive without a man to look after them. But he couldn't stay up here. He couldn't save the sheep. He wondered if he would be able to save himself.

He still had his clasp knife in his pocket. He began skinning the nearest carcass, thanking the saints that sheep were not tight-skinned animals like a horse or a pig. After he had pulled five hides—surely enough to keep himself warm and to make pampooties that would save his disintegrating boots—he began slicing the meat thin.

The dog was whimpering, but would not touch even a dead sheep until Paddy cut out a liver and flung it. Once food had received the blessing of human hands the dog ate. The boy festooned rocks with drying meat, then went upstream from where dead sheep were damming the tiny creek. It was midafternoon now and the clouds had parted momentarily. He stripped off his clothes and tried to scrub with handfuls of sand. But his body was too tender, too uniformly black and blue. He did what he could and climbed back into his reeking clothes, once more slipping on his gentleman's waistcoat over everything else. The hacking coat had disappeared somewhere during his mad flight last night. Coming back toward camp, he saw one of the donkeys. It had been shot.

The boy turned to the dog. "You know this country," he said. "Tell me now—would an Indian be shootin' a donkey? Or would he be stealin' it like any horse that's not lame or nailed down?"

The dog pondered the question but did not volunteer an opinion. Paddy remembered the old man's hints of a three-way competition over grass, but the boy just couldn't believe it. All this open country . . . he had not seen a single cow for over a month.

It was late afternoon and the buzzards were working up courage to land near dead sheep, pick cautiously at an eye, ready to fly at the slightest flutter of life. The boy knew he ought to be on his way but he was so sore and, besides, the meat was not dry.

The single collie had run himself ragged all day long, bringing the scattered remnants of the herd together to bed them down. Finally boy and dog lay down for the night.

Immediately Paddy knew it had been a mistake to stay here. With darkness every coyote, fox, and wolf in the territory converged on the dead sheep. He spent half the night feeding the fire, throwing blazing brands at those who came near his drying meat until finally they got it through their vulpine heads that the predators were to do their own butchering. The dog, who would have put up more of a defense if the other dogs had been alive, sensibly stuck close to Paddy and the fire.

Finally dawn came and thanks to fire and pulled skins, the boy had spent an uncomfortable but at least a warm night. He went from rock to rock collecting meat. It was not really dry, but in this chill, incredibly dry air the slices had formed a dry outer skin. He wrapped the meat in one of the hides and began braiding wide straps of the fragile, easily torn skin. By the time the sun was up he had created a pack and was walking downhill away from sheep, from scavengers, from everything.

But what was he walking into? The dog was torn between Paddy and the sheep. So was Paddy. He shouldn't be abandoning them. The old man had taken him in, probably saved his life. He owed him something. But the old Scotsman had shown neither sentiment nor loyalty to his charges. Had to be dead, Paddy guessed. Otherwise the old man would have reappeared by now.

Paddy felt bad about leaving the sheep but he had little choice. He reminded himself that if he were to save them he could easily end up jailed or hanged for stealing them. And as for their absentee owner . . . absentee ownership had caused most of Ireland's troubles. Paddy felt no obligation to some stranger who would appear at irregular intervals to lower wages and raise rents. He would see to the owner's interests just as soon as he finished selling an egg to Captain Boycott.

"You'd best be comin' with me now," he told the dog, and went on blathering the nonsense horses and sometimes women find agreeable. "Go on livin' up here without a man to feed you and all these sheep around and some hungry day you'll go forgettin' your holy vows and end up a killer."

After some soul-searching, Dorrga gave up and decided to follow Paddy.

Walking, after the trampling Paddy had taken, was sheer torment, but he didn't want to spend another night this close to so many wolves and coyotes. Besides, in spite of the cool, dry weather, carcasses were beginning to swell. Every time a scavenger punctured one the boy was reminded of the steerage where he had traveled while his gentleman occupied quarters more appropriate to his station in life—which now gave Paddy a small secret smile for, no matter how exalted his station, Paddy's gentleman no longer had any life. Paddy was black and blue, near barefoot, and alone in the world. "But I've got forty pounds of meat on me back," he told Dorrga. "And I've even got me a dog to talk to!"

They moved away from the skyful of buzzards, down into a cañon where Paddy almost drank until he realized it had to be the same creek that was damned upstream with dead sheep. From time to time the cañon widened and he caught glimpses of open, gradually flattening country below. Down here the sparse, short-cropped grass was no longer green and the trees were thinning out. Paddy studied the stream beside him, wishing he had been able to make some kind of canteen before leaving camp.

But he hadn't. He decided to walk until he could no longer bear the thirst. Didn't they all say it only took sixty feet for running water to purify itself? But they said a lot of things Paddy already knew were not true. He bore with his thirst. Never having been exposed to modern science, the dog drank when he pleased.

They walked all that day, following the stream until it widened from the contributions of two other small branches. The boy drank from these. He found enough dry wood to build a small, nearly smokeless fire and broil strips of partially dried mutton. Paddy guessed it might be more tasty if he had a bit of salt, but the dog did not complain about his portion.

Next morning they began walking again. It was nearing noon before they saw another sign of life. Compared to the sleek Irish kine, who always had first gleaning of the corn in a hierarchy that traditionally allowed cows, then sheep, then pigs, and finally the Irish into a given field, this rangy creature seemed scarcely worthy of the name of cow.

She was a longer-legged, more athletic-appearing beast who seemed incapable of producing any measurable quantity of milk. Her backbone was knobbed with warbles and her haunches with botflies, her eyes and nostrils with other parasites. But none of these defects seemed sufficient to alter an innately evil nature. The cow lowered her head and charged.

Paddy was wrapped in raw sheepskins and encumbered with a pack of half-dried meat. From his viewpoint it was obvious that the horns would be arriving first.

Chapter 6

As horns approached with the certitude of a vengeful god, Paddy had little time to ponder the irony that had protected him from an Indian raid and saved him from a massacre of the other sheep, only to see him done in by an outlaw cow. But this was so totally unjust that it never even occurred to the boy that now was a proper time for prayer. Instead, he began a Calling Down of Thunder upon the Bearded Ladies who wove and spun such gross inequities into the fabric of being. Obviously, the three weird sisters were in the pay of the British.

The collie's approach was more practical. He charged like a snarling black cannonball and locked onto the cow's muzzle, where he swung like a pendulum. He let go only when the cow turned to give Paddy a view of her hindquarter brand that, to his limited reading ability, looked very like the £ sign for pounds sterling. The dog dropped from the cow's muzzle, rolled once, then attached himself to her hindquarters until the cow's repentance seemed sincere.

When he came back Paddy embraced the collie who, being Scotch, seemed slightly embarrassed at such effusions. While he waited for strength to return to his legs, Paddy redid the pack and divested himself of the sheepskins. Down at this altitude it was becoming positively warm. He saw his second pounds-sterling cow an hour later, but this time the boy's nose forewarned him. Its legs pointed skyward. He was not anxious to pass downwind, but the boy was still a day or two short of sixteen and could not resist throwing a rock, which made the stiffening hide reverberate like the drum of a regimental band. In response a large ratlike creature emerged from the cow, followed by several offspring. When the dog approached they all promptly rolled over to play possum. Paddy crossed one entry from his list of possible edibles.

The smell from his pack was growing stronger, so that afternoon the boy camped early and rigged drying racks of willow saplings that grew in the creek bottom. He got a fire going and put the racks close around it. This time the wood was a little more damp and the fire smoked.

He hoped the brisk breeze would dissipate smoke before it could draw more of those nonexistent Indians. While the meat half dried, half roasted, he explored farther and found another branch. Where the creeks joined was a small space where the poplars had been cut down, with unmistakable signs that somebody had been planning on settling there. But for reasons unknown to Paddy, the project had been abandoned before the sill of the cabin was fair laid.

The creek itself was puzzling down here. Paddy had studied its sere, dry-grassed banks for some time before he understood that it was not a year-round flow, like the burns of home. This stream must have been dry all summer long and had only revived during the prolonged rainy spell that had plagued his gentleman's hunting in the mountains. In the last day the boy had passed two small dams, though he would have called them weirs. They were not the casual creations of those scaly-tailed animals that gnawed down trees. Still, the boy had been reluctant to admit that these barrages and the fresh pools of still water behind them could be man-made. Indians didn't build weirs. Thoughtfully, he finished kicking at the unfinished cabin and returned upstream to look to his drying meat.

Should have gone back sooner, he guessed. The collie had followed him and if the smell of that meat was drifting as far downwind as he supposed, there would be coyotes before long. He decided that if he hurried he could gather up everything and move a few odorless miles before settling down for the night. Then as they came closer the dog's hackles rose.

Paddy could smell nothing, and he almost misunderstood the warning. He gathered a half-dozen rocks and was ready to storm the spot when a caution born of the past few days warned him. He crept closer and saw that it was not coyotes stealing his meat. A man lay propped on one elbow before the fire, scoffing down a slice of half-dried, half-roasted, and totally unsalted mutton.

Indian? He was most assuredly not a white man, but he was wearing a hat and trousers. The dog growled, and immediately the intruder spun and fired a pistol in their general direction. Paddy replied with a rock whose aim was more accurate. It hit the stranger in the middle of his wide forehead. As the man slumped the boy ran forward and picked up the pistol. It was somewhat like the Bisley Colt his gentleman had bought for this American expedition but differed in some particulars—notably in that this Peacemaker had seen hard usage. He was still examining the gun when a huge fist closed over his ankle.

As he went down he managed with one wild swing to club the barrel of the Peacemaker over its owner's head. But it seemed a particularly hard head. The stranger grunted but did not release his grip. They thrashed for a moment and then Paddy was pinned.

And thus it came about that a sixteen-year-old Irish groom was getting ready to amputate the riddled foot of a black man who had most certainly helped kill the old Scotsman. Paddy held up the boot and looked at the older man through the three-quarter-inch hole of a Tower musket ball. "Will ye be tellin' me there's another gun like it in this territory?"

It seemed the other man would not be.

"Is it hurtin' you are?"

"I've known better days."

" 'Twill be nice to look back on them, for ye've few to look forward to."

"Hard," the black man muttered. "What I ever do to you?"

Paddy rolled up his sleeve. "See thim black-and-blue marks? All over me they are. I'll do me job and take your foot off, but 'tis no tears I'm sparin' for them would bury me under tons o' sheep. And I'll thank yez nivver to call *me* hard again!"

The black glared and for an instant it looked like he would struggle against the lariat. Then he looked away. "Oh," he said.

Paddy felt like saying more but there was not that much more to say. If he were to let himself be drawn into talk this man would deny it all and the longer he talked the more convincing he would become, and soon the boy would be believing it was all a big mistake, that this territory was overflowing with Tower muskets and other relics of the Napoleonic wars, that the black man had never been within a hundred miles of where the Scotsman blew his foot near off, that none of it had ever really happened and that he, Paddy, was just imagining all those aches and pains, those bruises on his lacerated body. "And next ye'll be tellin' me 'tis beef ye're stealin' from me!"

The boy had performed the usual brutal surgeries on horses but, apart from digging out an occasional thorn or sliver, he had never practiced on his own species. The longer he thought about it the more worried he became. Though he owed this murderer nothing, to leave him to his own devices was one thing. To kill him was another. The Church was definite about that.

And even if he were not to slip into mortal sin, Paddy knew it was going to become very untidy once he began working his knife between bones he had felt in his own ankle but never actually seen. If the black man were to start thrashing he could easily botch it. The boy's hardness evaporated.

"'Tis up to you," he repeated, praying the other would change his mind.

But the boy's arguments had either soaked in, or had reinforced what the black man must have known all the time: In 1881 even the most up-to-date Edinburgh surgeons would not dream of salvaging this shattered mass of pus and bones. "Go ahead," he sighed.

Paddy took a deep breath and laid the flame-witched knife where the blade would not touch anything while he rolled up the pants leg above the shattered foot. "Jaysus, Mary, and Joseph!" he muttered.

The swelling was halfway up the calf, skin taut and black, save where veins were rimmed in red. Paddy remembered the last time he had seen a leg like that—when a neighbor had sent word to his father days after a mishap with a scythe. Paddy's father in those days had been head groom and nearest thing to a surgeon for the Catholic constituency of the eastern shore of Lough Neagh. Himself had removed a leg but the patient had died.

"What's wrong?" the black man demanded.

"Too late."

If he had argued, Paddy knew he would have washed his hands of the whole business. But the black man didn't. "Oh," he said quietly.

"It's halfway to your knee," the boy said. "'Twould be easier to part the joint there."

There was a moment of silence and then the black man said, "No."

Paddy was about to tell him there was no chance unless he cut it off, when he changed his mind. Instead, he began untying the huge man, still keeping his careful distance and working from behind.

"You leavin'?"

"I'll stay." Perversely, now that he had gotten out of it, Paddy was obsessed with the idea that he might have performed a successful amputation. "I can still try."

"No!" the black man snarled. "A man makes his livin'

ridin' a horse. You think I want to be jus' another darkie—'nother po' ol' uncle swampin' out the bunkhouse, doin' all the nigger work? Man gits tired of bein' called a boy."

"Doesn't sound all that different from being Irish," Paddy grumped.

"Like hell it don't! Boy, you git a haircut an' some clean clothes an' you a gentleman. Ain't nothin' ever gonna make me white."

Paddy remembered the gulf that had separated him from his gentleman. Was it truly that easy to rise in this country? He finished untying the black man and returned to his own side of the fire, where he pulled a withie from his drying rack and spitted a piece of mutton. Would he ever see salt again, or bread, or a cup of tea? The collie lay at his feet, scrupulously avoiding the drying racks but waiting with mournful eyes for the boy to feed him.

"You didn't do it alone," Paddy reflected. "Why'd your friends leave you here?"

"Reckon they figured I got killed like the others."

Paddy's ears pricked up. Had the old Scotsman managed to get more than one of them with his muzzle-loading relic? He remembered to his chagrin that he had not buried the old man—hadn't even made a proper search for him. But even now he still ached in every joint, and if he weren't careful one of those punctures would turn into the same kind of blood poisoning that was running up the black man's leg.

They sat facing each other across the fire, each obsessed with his own dark thoughts. "How long you been in this country?" the black finally asked.

Paddy wasn't sure. He explained about his gentleman's hunting trip and ended up with the story of the swollen-jawed Indian.

"Lumpjaw!" the black muttered.

Paddy stared and waited but no more information was forthcoming. "You ain't goin' home again," the black said. "So what you plannin' on doin' now?"

Paddy had never seen such a country for people wanting to know his plans. Until very recently the boy had not even known the meaning of the word. Now it seemed—to everyone else at least—as if his entire future depended on whatever he decided to do in the next hour or day.

The creekbank had gradually risen until it was uncomfortably close to drying racks and the fire. Paddy wondered if it was a new storm or if it had taken all this time for the rain that had plagued him and his gentleman to fill all the dams between here and the mountains. "Can you walk?" he asked.

"I can hop but that gits old in a hurry. Reckon I could make it that far," the black man added when he saw in which direction Paddy was looking.

But Paddy's plans were more elaborate. He described the beginnings of a cabin downstream a hundred yards. "No roof or anything but it's higher ground and there's enough cut logs to make a lean-to if it decides to rain again."

"Snow'd be more like it," the black growled. "Cabin, you say?"

"In the midst of a lot of poplars—where another creek forks into this one."

"Well I'll be damned!"

"Murderers always are," Paddy agreed.

The black man ignored his comment. "Didn't know I was that close."

"Close to what?"

"He was jus' some squatter. Run him out years ago."

"And why did you do that?"

The black man gave him the look one gives to someone who's not all there. "He was stealin' our water."

"Your water? You're God? Did you make the creek?"

"No, boy. I don' need nobody to explain the works of God and man. But it 'pears like you do."

Paddy waited.

"You walked this watercourse down from the mountains, didn't you?"

Paddy nodded.

"And all them dams you saw—all them pools of water behin' them. You think it was God come up here with a four-horse team and a fresno and scraped up all that dirt? You think God done bust his back pilin' up stonework facing, diggin' spillways, and comin' back up here every fall repairin' all them tanks to git ready for nex' year's runoff? Boy, you ever see God doin' that you let me know, 'cause I ain't never seed him string a fence or brand a calf or dig out a screwworm or even git up to light a fire on a cold morning. You find me a god can keep a man's feet warm—or keep this'n from rottin' off—and boy, you got yourself a believer."

Now that Paddy reflected on it, his Creator had never really been one to pitch in with the chores, even back in God's Own Country. "Did you build all those weirs yourself?" he asked.

"'Course not. But I ride for the Bar L what done it. Old Bill Lawson first come to this country, he only had me and a couple of no-'count white men couldn't 'member the war's over. They wasn't sleepin' in the same tent with no nigger, so Bill sent 'em down the trail. Tol' 'em if they ever saw another nigger could rope like this'n, to send him by. If they was any God 'round here in them days he must've been bettin' on the Indians. Sure never done us no favors."

Paddy was still studying the creek. "Can you do a hundred yards with your arm around my shoulder?"

"Might be I could."

Paddy helped the black to his feet. He got a firebrand but it burned out long before they had hobbled all the way to the abandoned cabinsite. He felt around in the darkness and made the black as comfortable as possible amid the leaves. Then he went back upstream to bring fire and the rest of their meager supplies.

He was tired and still far from over all the harms done him by sheep and Indians, but Paddy supposed the black man was worse off. He could not bring himself to make even a murderer suffer more. He got the black bedded down on sheepskins in a corner of the cabin's beginning and started another fire. It was growing colder with each minute.

There was no way the boy was going to build a cabin without tools, but he managed to prop up a ridgepole and lay a few sticks over it to make a lean-to and keep in some tiny portion of the fire. When he had roofed it with sheepskins it was almost pleasant inside. The black man drifted into an uneasy sleep. Untroubled by his conscience, Paddy slept more profoundly.

With morning he discovered the black had awakened often enough to keep the fire going. At first the boy thought it had snowed; then he saw it was only a thick hoarfrost that covered everything. He walked off into the brush to do what boys usually do on first arising. When he returned the black man was gone.

Same errand, Paddy supposed. He busied himself with spreading the remaining meat out for drying, repeatedly walking the hundred yards back and forth from his previous campsite to salvage the withies of his drying rack. An hour passed and the black man was still missing.

"Serves him right," the boy muttered, "and bad cess to all murderers." But that did not keep him from exploring the poplars that filled the fork, describing ever greater circles until he found the black man sitting hunched a few hundred yards upstream from his horse. "And don't yez think I've better ways t' spend me time than lookin' all mornin' for the likes of you?" he demanded.

The black man gave him an odd look but after a moment struggled to his feet and let the boy help him back to the lean-to and fire. The boy knew he ought to be on his way down out of these mountains but he could not bring himself to desert the only other human in these parts.

He wished for a pot, for tea, for salt, for any number of things he did not have. He needed an ax, but wishing did not seem to produce tangible results. To keep warm and prevent his bruised body from getting any stiffer, the boy poked about the clearing, ripping branches from the poplars. The leaves were changing color but enough of them stayed on the branches for him to rig a better roof to their lean-to.

The black man lay in silent misery before the fire. He was no longer hungry. Paddy preferred not to look at the shapeless, moribund mass at the end of his swollen leg. He was tempted to I-told-you-so's but managed to control himself. When he had roofed the lean-to and piled brush at both ends to make a relatively enclosed place before the fire he tended the drying racks, turning the now stiff slabs of mutton. He had started out with over forty pounds. There was less than half that weight now, thanks to evaporation and the appetites of a man, a boy, and a dog. "How far is it to town?" he asked.

The black aroused himself from some private vision to stare, and for a moment the boy thought he had gone round the bend. Then intelligence returned to those black eyes. "Ain't no town around here, boy," he said. "Nearest town's two hundred miles. You need anything in these parts you goes to ol' Bill Lawson's big house."

"The man who killed the sheep?"

"The man who fought off the Indians so he could run cattle in this country." The black man studied Paddy from fever-bright eyes. "And, boy, you want to git along 'round here, you gits along with Bill Lawson. He gittin' old and kinda set in his ways. You go 'round his place stinkin' of sheep an' you jus' ain' gonna git along."

Paddy sat before the fire digesting this information long after the other man had drifted back into a sleep from which he occasionally muttered in accents so different from the English of Paddy's region that the boy assumed it was some other language.

If he had a brain in his head he'd be on his way. Two hundred miles . . . move out now and there was still a hope of making it before the snow came—while he still had some meat left. With luck he might even catch a stray horse. According to Mr. Bridgeman this country was overrun with strays, although the boy had yet to see a horse without a brand and a rider.

But which way was town? That lumpy-jawed Indian had warned him away from Fort Rudge. He resolved to ask the black man for more detailed directions, once he was awake again. But for now the boy was tired and it was warm near the fire.

While he slept Paddy dreamed that he was home with his little brothers poking and prodding for their share of the blankets. Twice he almost came awake enough to fight back, but it wasn't until he heard a distant shot that the boy struggled up out of sleep. The black man was gone again. So was the pistol the boy had taken from him. Once more Paddy knew somebody had taken decision out of his hands. He got up and began circling, knowing this time what he was going to find.

Chapter 7

The first thing Paddy discovered was ice rimming the creek this morning. The iron-hard ground was rimed with hoarfrost. He stamped along in worn boots, once more describing a widening spiral around the campsite until he found the black man. The Colt was still in one frozen hand. The boy removed it, then knelt and crossed himself.

He prayed briefly for the black man's soul and went into greater detail concerning any possible liability for his own sins of commission or omission. He couldn't get it straight in his mind whether the black man was really all the villain that murder and sheep killing would make him out to be. Unbidden, the Scots herder's words came to mind: "'Tis a cruel world, lad. If ye dinna' learn that ye're no' long for it." Paddy feared he might have to learn to be harder than the black man had been.

He wondered if the wounded man had been doing him a favor—or doing himself one. Either way the boy was no longer saddled with that responsibility.

He kicked at the frozen ground. Not too hard, lest his boots finish coming apart. A stone came loose and he picked it up. It was an arrowhead. Paddy studied it and wondered if some explorer of an unknown race might someday paw the shards of one of his mother's teacups and wonder what kind of man lived in Ireland back in the days Before Sheep. Was he walking on some Indian's grave?

He sighed. Soon the coyotes would get to the black man. He could build fires and pick away at the inch or two of thawed ground but that could take all winter. He struggled to close staring, death-clouded eyes, could not prevail against rigor mortis, and finally pulled a Stetson down over the black face.

He spent the next couple of hours piling boulders over the body and finally knelt once more to say a Salve Regina, which the boy could recite in Latin or in Irish. It had never occurred to him that prayers might also be rendered in the Devil's Tongue. Finished, he returned to the lean-to and near-dead fire. It took a good half hour to get feeling back into his numb hands and feet, and then they tingled so that he wished they were numb again.

He picked at a piece of shoe-leather-hard mutton and shared it with the dog, who—like a good Irish groom, Paddy suddenly realized—was too well-trained to grab a fair share even if the drying racks were in plain sight and reach. He sat in the lean-to chewing and envying the dog who, after a few perfunctory efforts, scoffed down his share whole.

Paddy had never been a geographer. Never been anything but a groom. He could write his name and sometimes guess at signs but that was the size of it. Still, the notion had somehow entered his head that towns were often on rivers and that rivers, in Christian countries at least, tend to flow downhill.

Since the lumpy-jawed Indian had dissuaded him from going down the other side of the mountains, Paddy had been steadily descending this side. As long as he kept moving downhill, downstream, sooner or later the boy was sure he would find a town. All he had to do was stay alive, stay fed, shod, and out of Bill Lawson's way.

Sheepskins with the wool on are warm enough, but their tensile strength, no matter how well tanned, is midway between a slice of fresh soda bread and a bowl of cottage cheese. The boy poked among the poplars and found a thorny bush. If he'd had a nail or a piece of wire to heat red hot in the fire his needle could have had an eye in it but there was no iron to spare. Then he remembered the saddle upstream. Ought to be a ring or buckle on it.

And the rawhide lariat was a better source of sewing material than he would ever find trying to spin uncombed wool. He went upstream. It was so cold the gut-shot horse had not even started to swell. He undid the cinch and struggled but could not work it free. Finally he cut the saddle loose and brought it back to the lean-to. It took most of the day to fashion sleeves onto one skin and thongs to tie it round him. Once finished making a coat, the boy struggled to fashion pampooties against the day his boots disintegrated.

The dog studied the leaden sky and whined. If he'd thought it would do any good, Paddy would have whined too. Instead, he gathered dry wood and bedded down for another night in the lean-to. Before going to sleep he rechecked the Colt, which he had recovered. He removed the one empty cartridge and fiddled with the single-action mechanism until he thought he had the hang of it. He reloaded the gun. When it was full he still had over a dozen cartridges left in his pocket. Tomorrow he would punch a new hole in that belt and make the holster fit around his considerably smaller waist.

But when morning came Paddy realized he was going to have to rethink his situation again. It was not so bitter cold now as it had been all day yesterday. But this morning the fork was buried under a foot and a half of soft, wet snow. The lean-to of leafy branches had sagged under the weight until he could only get out by wriggling wormlike past the sodden remains of the campfire.

The boy tried to be philosophical. He had known it would snow sooner or later. Better caught here with some kind of windbreak among the dense poplars—with at least this poor excuse for a roof, and not out in the open, where life could turn so miserable that it might no longer even be life.

He wondered if there were fish in this creek, and if it would be possible to weave a weir of withies and chase them into it, as was sometimes done at home providing there was an extra boy could keep an eye out for the steward and the gamekeeper.

Whoever had started to build this cabin had possessed a keen appreciation of the site. Water, grass, shelter from wind and sun. If a man had to spend a winter here, Paddy guessed he could do worse.

The mutton might last him and the dog another three weeks. Fish? Game? Sheep? A cow? He wondered if antelope like the old Scotsman had killed would range this far down out of the mountains. But mostly, the boy wondered about Indians.

He had lived so long without tea that he hardly missed it any longer. He got to his feet and plowed with some difficulty through knee-deep snow looking for any novelty. There were pheasant and quail tracks. There were also what looked like hare tracks, save that they were twice as long as any he'd ever seen. "So what would that be now?" he asked. The dog sniffed at jackrabbit tracks but made no comment. Paddy went back to the lean-to, where he braided a snare. Common sense told him there were neither gamekeepers nor penalties for poaching in these parts. Still, the boy couldn't feel easy about it.

That night the moon came out bright and clear. As he lay warm in his skins waiting for sleep to come, Paddy heard the tiny whistling shriek that meant fresh meat. He was tempted to leave it till morning but he supposed the coyotes would not be so patient.

The dog followed him through the poplars to where he had strung the snare. Paddy was disentangling the rabbit when he heard a noise so familiar that for a moment he paid no attention. Then suddenly the boy was galvanized. Somewhere downstream, echoing up the leafy tunnel of the creekbed, he could hear the heavy breathing of a horse.

Jesus, Mary, and Joseph—His Lordship's gamekeeper! Then the boy remembered where he was. Why hadn't he finished up before dark? Why hadn't he punched another hole in that belt so he would have the pistol with him now? He dropped the rabbit and sprinted back to camp, waving the dog to silence with a gesture he had learned from the Scotsman.

It took the boy a moment to realize that despite his carelessness, Something was still looking after him. He reached the lean-to, snatched up the gun and as much else as he could carry, and made a beeline back into the brush. The horse noise was louder now. Lucky he'd been out recovering a rabbit, for if he'd been back down at the cabinsite the murmur of the icebound creek might have left him unwarned.

The wind was down off the mountains, which meant the sour, sappy smell of Paddy's poplar fire was drifting straight toward the horseman. It was only one horse; he was sure of that. The Indian? The boy draped the gunbelt over his shoulder, pending daylight and time to poke another hole. He checked the loaded Colt, mentally drilling himself in the way the hammer had to be pulled back and marveling at the ingenuity with which this simple act revolved the cylinder and placed another round ready to fire. He wondered if the lumpy-jawed Indian would find it as amusing to be on the receiving end of hard times.

He lay shivering in the darkness. Not from cold, thanks to skins, which gave him the appearance of an oddly proportioned sheep, but from the excitement of being for once in control of his fate. This time nobody was going to sneak up and surprise him. Indian, white, or devil, Paddy's pistol was loaded and he was ready. "Lord God of hosts," he whispered, "smite mine enemies."

From time to time he could hear the horse snort but it progressed so slowly that he began to doubt. Could this be the answer to his prayers? No ridden horse would dawdle along and take half an hour to reach him. If the horse had no rider, maybe he could catch it.

He started sneaking back once more toward the campfire and the lariat—now a yard shorter from all his sewing, but still several times as long as anything he had ever used in Ireland to toll a horse.

It was tricky. The campsite in the cabin's quadrangle was closer to the creek, and the water made just enough noise for him not to hear the horse's heavy breathing as it tramped over windfalls and through snow. But if this horse were to be as skittish as all those he had tended in his gentleman's string, the boy knew he must have some rope.

Why couldn't he have thought of it in the first place instead of panicking and grabbing the pistol, meat, sheepskins, everything except the rawhide lariat he was going to need? The horse had to be used to humans or it would not be following the smoke toward oats or whatever fire builders fed their mounts in this country.

Paddy dithered in a positive agony of indecision. It was acting like a riderless horse. He was willing to swear there was only one animal out there. But mistakes in this country seemed to turn out even more costly than at home.

He ought to be making a dash for the lean-to and lariat—not hovering here at the edge of the tiny clearing straining his ears and trying to make up his mind. But he could not force himself to break cover. Instead, he pulled back deeper into the poplars, up and away from the creek where once more he could hear the horse's blowing. Only this time it was behind him!

The fool beast was grazing, picking its random way as it pawed snow and hunted out patches of brown grass under windfalls. And he had thought it would be sniffing its way upwind to the fire, hungry for human companionship and handouts.

And then, just barely in time, Paddy realized how few times in his life he had ever known a horse to graze at night. For this horse to deviate from the trail of smoke that the beast associated with food and companionship could only mean that somebody was directing the horse back and forth across the thicket that lined the creek. Somebody was out hunting. Hunting Paddy!

He scooted back and hid among the half-leaved poplars only seconds before horse and rider drew in sight. The lean man on the bay was so muffled in clothing it was hard to make out more than a long-lipped, totally Irish-looking face. But now he was hot on the scent of the campfire and passed nearly within touch of Paddy without seeing him, ignoring his mount's sniff at the man-sheep reek that drifted downwind from the boy.

Paddy lay in darkness with the Colt aimed. But as the stranger came close and could actually see the campfire he turned cautious enough to slip from the saddle and leave his bay ground-tied just beyond the flicker of light.

The dismounted stranger circled the lean-to until he was on the opposite side and could see in. He moved closer. Paddy remembered the black man's warning about sneaking up on a camp in this country. With equal care the boy oozed from his own hiding place under the windfall. He described a wider circle through the brush, making for the ground-tied horse.

He was nearly there when the horse's nostrils swelled. It tossed its head and moved so close to the firelight that the boy didn't dare follow.

The long-lipped rider studied the raw sheepskin bed with obvious disgust. He picked up one stiffening hide and was about to toss it in the fire when abruptly he changed his mind. It took Paddy a moment to see what had caught the other man's attention. Then he saw that the long-lipped stranger was hunkered down over the saddle he had salvaged from the black man's horse.

He turned the saddle over, noting each ring or buckle Paddy had removed. He put it down. "Hey, Ottie!" he yelled, "Ottie, where in hell you hidin'? Come in here now. You hear?"

Paddy measured the triangle whose points were himself, the man at his campfire, and the horse. Part of his mind noted that the black man's name had been Ottie. Odd that he had never learned that. But then, you don't go exchanging cards with murderers.

If this Irish-faced man had come out here hunting the

black, then he had to be one of those who had done in the old Scotsman and the sheep. But was there any connection between these murderers and the long-haired Indian variety?

What difference did it make? Paddy could not sprint fast enough to mount the horse and be on his way before the other man could draw the huge pistol he wore. Even if he could, the boy didn't want to abandon the meat and sheepskins that had saved his life so far.

And where was the dog? As if in reply he heard a growl and then furious barking from the opposite side of the tiny clearing. But when the stranger stood his ground the dog subsided. His job was sheep and his enemies were four-legged.

"Ottie! Goldang it, it's me—Jug."

"Ottie's dead," Paddy said. Before saying it he made sure that when the intruder spun the first thing he would see was the muzzle of Ottie's pistol.

Chapter 8

For an instant Paddy thought he was going to have to shoot; then the long-lipped Jug thought better of going for his gun. "Who the hell are you?" he demanded.

"You forst."

"My God, an Irishman!" The stranger's face took on his sheepskin-handling look.

Paddy emitted a rapid gabble. If the long-lipped stranger understood, his face did not give him away. "Talk American!" he snarled.

"I was sayin' 'tis a great shame on you not to be talkin' Irish an' you wid a face like that."

"So who the hell are you and what'd you do with Brutus?"

"Minute ago you were callin' him Ottie."

The stranger's eyes narrowed momentarily and a hint of secret amusement entered him. "So I was now, wasn't I?"

Paddy was still wondering what was so funny about it when the lariat settled over his shoulders. As he felt himself being jerked backward the Colt went off, sending a foot of fire skyward and leaving his ears ringing.

Minutes later the boy crouched by the fire looking into the bores of two pistols. "Learn something new every day, don't you, boy?" the second man said. "My name's Ottie. Now what's yours?"

The boy told him, but since Patrick, in Irish, sounds more like Fawrig, neither man understood. "Where's Brutus?" they demanded.

"If you're meanin' a big black man, I offered to cut off his foot but instead he chose to cut off his life."

"Where is he?"

"I couldn't bury him. He's under a pile o' rocks out there." Gradually, with occasional encouragement from the toe of a high-heeled boot, Paddy told the story of his adventures with his gentleman and Mr. Bridgeman. He recalled the black man's warning. "And then I came across a ravine brimful of dead sheep," he abridged. "'Tis that kept me alive till your friend showed up with a rotten foot and a gut-shot horse. You'll find the beast a quarter league upstream if the animals've not finished him yet."

"And you don't know where he got shot or who did it?"

"He didn't tell me," Paddy said. Which, strictly speaking, was the truth. The dog emerged from the darkness and sat nervously at the edge of the firelight.

"Looks like a sheepdog," Ottie growled.

Paddy shrugged as best he could inside the loop of lariat. "'Tis there by the sheep he fixed onto me."

"He's not yours?"

"Everything o' mine I last saw leavin' along with a lumpy-jawed Indian."

"A what?"

Paddy glanced up as something swift passed between the two men. "What'd His Highness bring you over to this country for?" one asked.

"I'm a groom."

"You ain't old enough to be married!"

"I think he means he's a wrangler," the first man said.

"What do you know about horses?"

"I see one will never take you home unless you get that dirty pad off and let the sore heal. Ye'd best throw the filthy thing away and use one o' these skins with the wool side down."

"What sore?"

"Take the saddle off and look." The boy spoke with the serene assurance of a man who knows what he's talking about. The one called Jug glared for a moment, then went to unsaddle his mount. "Be goddamned," he muttered.

Paddy was sure they both already were but, tied up and between them, he was in no position to antagonize anyone.

"How'd you know he was gallin'?"

"I know horses," the boy said flatly. "I saw your nose curl at a sheepskin but his won't."

"You sure you didn't kill Brutus?"

"Would I have wasted me time buryin' him? D'ye think I'm fool enough to stay here and trap meself out wid all the things belonged to your dead friend? A man knows horses must needs be as smart as they are."

"Then why would he kill himself?"

"Told me he was a man on a horse, that he'd not be doin' a boy's work again."

Jug and Ottie looked at one another. "Sounds like Brutus all right," Jug said grudgingly. "So why'd you draw down on me?"

Once more Paddy quoted the black man. "And what do you expect when you come sneakin' up on me in the dark? You're not the first Indian's come traffickin'."

While they had been wrangling back and forth the boy had gradually worked himself free of the lariat. When he worked it over his shoulders and tossed it to one side neither man made to tie him up again. Instead, the two cowboys studied him thoughtfully. "What're you gonna do now, boy?" Jug asked.

The third time! Paddy wondered if Americans were just naturally nosy. Why was everyone so interested in his future? Until a week ago the boy had given it no more thought than does any well-fed horse. "I don't know," he said. "But 'tis not likely I'll be goin' back to County Down. No doubt there's somebody in this country could use a man knows how to keep a horse alive."

"Ain't it the truth," Ottie said mournfully. He produced a pint of whiskey from a saddlebag. "Was savin' that," he explained. "Thought Brutus might be needin' it. Reckon we need it worse." He swigged off a third and passed the bottle to Jug, who extracted his share before handing the bottle on to Paddy.

It was not the fiery, soul-warming poteen the boy had known at home, but this odd-tasting, Indian-corn spirit was the best he had tasted in over a week. Ottie unsaddled and hobbled his horse and the three of them crowded into the lean-to, where they burrowed into sheepskins.

"You sure you ain't gonna run off now, boy?" Ottie asked. "Steal a horse in this country and you'll hang."

Where Paddy came from a man would hang for stealing a sheep or a goat. "Where could I run?" he asked.

The older man surveyed him doubtfully. "I think I'll sleep better if I'm sure," he said, and tied the boy hand and foot before putting him to bed between the two of them.

"Not so tight," the boy complained. "Ye want me hands to fall off?"

Ottie obligingly slacked off a bit while Paddy strained to swell each muscle. Finally the men were snoring. Paddy struggled for hours. He could have been free in minutes if he had not been jammed in between two sleeping men but he was—so he sweated and strained and devised new torments for every speaker of the English tongue. Finally he was free. The sky was clear and starry now and he knew it would be a good day for traveling.

He wondered if it would be possible for him and the dog to get away with the horses before Jug and Ottie woke up. He was just about resolved to try when he changed his mind. So far, at least, these men had not tried to kill him. It was as good a reception as he had experienced anywhere in this country. So, instead of stealing everything loose and lighting out, the boy quietly tied their feet together. Then he went back to sleep.

He was awakened by the sound of one man rolling in the snow and the other sitting up still half asleep. Their language attained an ethereal realm of blasphemy far beyond the continual goddamning of his deceased gentleman. And most of it was directed at Paddy. He accepted their abuse, content in the knowledge that he had allayed any suspicions. Now they would not expect him to rob them and do a flit.

Both men resolutely refused the boy's jerked mutton, so he fed the dog some and the rest of them breakfasted on oats and coffee, both dressed with tinned milk. After the days of dried unsalted meat he was properly appreciative of oats but doubted if he would ever come to enjoy the bitter blackness that these men called coffee. It was, he decided, a proper brew for murderers.

There was a brief pilgrimage to the black man's mound of stones, where Jug and Ottie removed their hats for a brief instant but made no other propitiatory gestures. Paddy had done enough praying. He took turns riding pillion with both men all that day as the horses plowed through the snow, bloodying pasterns and cannons from the sharp crust.

That evening, while the men got a fire going in the line cabin, the boy cut strips of sheepskin and wrapped them like leggins with the greasy wool against the horses' abraded legs. It might be months, he had learned, before they would ride to the bunkhouse and report to old Bill Lawson, who was bound to feel put out when he learned old Brutus was dead. Paddy stood in the clear evening air looking at the horses and the open country that stretched for endless miles downhill, downriver, down to where sooner or later there had to be a town. It would be so easy to leave these assassins stranded here. . . .

But as smoke and other savory smells emanated from the line cabin, the boy knew he was not going to do it. He held the door open against Jug and Ottie's protests until the dog came in too.

It's a new world and new rules, the boy told himself. A hard world too, and if he didn't learn to keep his mouth shut he'd not be long for it. These two men had most probably been out on the sheep-killing expedition with the black man. Gotten separated when the old Scotsman's Tower musket had been unexpectedly effective. But they had come back looking for the black man. More than anyone had ever done so far for Paddy. Perhaps there were degrees of evil even among murderers.

But good or evil, they knew the country. Paddy didn't. There was something about this pair of simple-minded assassins that fascinated the boy and he couldn't tell exactly what it was. The one called Jug had a totally Irish face and no memory of his origins. Chances were he would turn out to have a name like Murphy blissfully coupled with an attitude of No Irish Need Apply. Ottie was darker, with a skin that had been white before half a lifetime in sun and wind. But his hair and four-day growth of whiskers were black as a Protestant's soul.

Jug was dishing up bowls of slumgullion and the boy was again amazed that this man could use so many Irish words and never guess their origin. They scoffed down the stew and fed the dog, who thanked the two men with a stiff and totally Scots reserve. The boy went outside to scrub the dishes with clean chunks of crusty snow. He came back into the welcome warmth and began putting the dishes into the saddlebags for tomorrow's journey—and found the black man's Peacemaker, which they had taken away from him.

Silently, the boy swung the cylinder out of the empty revolver and began cleaning it the way the old Scotsman had taught him with the Tower musket. Jug and Ottie glanced at one another but neither said anything as the boy finished oiling and wiping the huge Colt. He loaded it and put it on the table.

"Not that way," Jug said.

Paddy looked at him.

"If your horse buckjumps and knocks the hammer down on a live one, you'll blow your foot off just like—"

It took the boy an instant to understand what the older man meant; then he took one bullet out and turned the cylinder until any accident would bring the hammer down on God's clean air. He took the huge belt and the rock and nail that the line cabin's kitchen kept for opening milk tins. As the older men watched him fit the black man's belt to his waist they seemed suddenly much too sentimental for murderers.

"He was a friend to yez?" the boy asked.

"He was," Jug said gruffly and became very busy twisting up a cigarette.

"Old Brutus—he was a reg'lar jim-dandy," Ottie said. Neither man seemed inclined to say more.

Paddy tried on the belt. Even for his oversized hands the pistol was heavy and awkward. He wondered if he would ever get the hang of drawing it smoothly without snagging the sight or dropping it as his thumb struggled to pull that high hammer back. But even more, he wondered if either of these near-blubbering assassins had any suspicion of what he would someday do with this gun. He glanced at the collie and suddenly suspected those unwinking eyes understood him perfectly. But then, the dog and his master had come from Scotland, where the memories of old hatreds are at least as long as those of Ireland.

"What you plannin' on doin' with that there pistol?" Jug asked.

The boy barely managed not to drop it. Struggling for a casual air, he said, "If I'd had it a few days ago I might not have so many holes in me. And an Indian might have a few in him. Could be even my gentleman and Mr. Bridgeman would still be alive."

"Bridgeman?"

Paddy nodded.

"Little squinty-eyed feller in greasy buckskin?"

"And no hair on the top of his head."

"That couldn't be Bridgeman," Ottie interjected.

"Would ye be layin' a shilling on it?"

Ottie studied the boy for a moment. "Old Shorty lost his hair? Be danged if it don't make a man think."

Paddy had thought of little else for something over a week. He busied himself packing everything that would not be needed for morning biscuits and coffee. Here in the cabin there were extra blankets in the bunks that lined one wall—heavy woolens the men persisted in calling soogans. They were emphatic in insisting he use the soogans and leave his ripening sheepskins outside.

The boy argued and complained. Not that he gave a damn, but he didn't want them to realize that he already had what he really wanted. Once he had seen the big house of their estate and learned the lay of the land downriver . . .

But sweet as revenge may be, after a long day in the cold, slumber is sweeter. He was nearly asleep before he understood, partly at least, what it was about Jug and Ottie that had kept him from killing them already. They were the first who had not tried to tell him there weren't any Indians around here.

Chapter 9

Paddy didn't know what he had been expecting from Jug and Ottie but it certainly was not this. Had he been overestimating his importance? He was, after all, only a groom, and even if the gentry of these parts saw fit to take note of him, they could not be expected to waste any of their precious time on a lost boy.

But it had been over a week since he had been "rescued" by this pair of assassins, and so far their master had not even had an opportunity to learn of Paddy's existence. He had thought their journey would continue back down to the great house but instead, now that the black man no longer needed assistance, Jug and Ottie had settled down to winter routine at the line cabin.

It was too late in the season and the ground too flinty to dig postholes but they rode out each day to stretch more barbed wire. Between times they shagged an occasional stray back within the pale, which stretched in an endless straight line farther than the boy could see.

Each man had possessed an extra mount, but while they had been out looking for the black man the horses had finished chewing through the top pole of the corral, so now they had only the horses they had ridden, which left the boy afoot. He sifted through the line cabin's treasures and found little apart from some powdered sulfur. He dusted the galled horse's back daily until the sore scabbed over.

The sheepskin he had substituted for the filth-encrusted saddle blanket was rapidly matting down. One day he boiled enough water to temper the chill in the watering trough so he could soak the old saddle blanket in tepid water and ashes. It hung stiff as a Scotsman's pride for a week over the top rail of the corral, but when the saddle blanket finally freeze-dried, it was soft and weighed half as much. If he'd had a change, he might have done as much for his tattering tweeds. But it was much too cold to live without trousers.

Then one night it rained and the snow melted half away. Next morning the crust was even more murderous for horses, so Jug and Ottie stuck to the cabin, splitting and piling wood as they made bets on how soon it would snow again. Toward nightfall it began sifting down light and dry, so Ottie won.

After a day out in the winter both men would strip down to their long-handled underwear and keep the cabin's interior so hot that the boy, who was from a country where wool is more abundant than fuel, had to dash outside from time to time for a few breaths of the totally dehydrated air of an American winter. His lips were cracking and the inside of his head had a shrunken, brittle feel. But invariably, each time the boy stuck his head outside Jug and Ottie would chorus their "Close that goddamn door!"

Two days after the second snowfall the runaway horses were waiting when Paddy opened the door for a hasty airing out before his rescuers could awaken and complain. He got into his disintegrating boots and corraled the beasts.

He was frying flapjacks when Ottie picked up the stick that bore a notch for each day. Paddy had not noticed their primitive calendar until he had been at the cabin long enough to have lost track. But Jug too was intent on the notches. They looked at one another. Ottie nodded.

"That galled horse about healed?" he asked.

"Are we goin' somewhere?" Paddy asked.

"Have to move out pretty soon now."

"Where's your Christmas spirit?" Jug asked.

"I've not had a drop," Paddy said. He hadn't realized so much time had passed. Anyhow, Christmas in Ireland had never been much apart from an extra Mass and an extra callus on his knees. "You'd travel in this weather just for a holiday?" he asked.

"Don't believe I would," Ottie said. "Anyways, near's I make it, Christmas must've come day before yesterday."

"How old are you, Pistol?" Jug asked.

Paddy had at first thought they were making fun of the loving care he devoted to the dead black man's Peacemaker, but finally Jug had explained that Pistol was this country's name for a boy who did a man's work for a man's pay. And he was still not sure about the wages. "Something over sixteen," Paddy guessed.

"You're a few days over twenty-one," Jug said. "And don't you go forgettin' it."

At Paddy's age there are obvious advantages in showing this kind of recklessness with vital statistics, so he accepted the amendment without comment. "But if you missed Christmas, why would yez be goin' anywheres now?"

"New Year's," Ottie said.

When he saw that no more information was going to be volunteered the boy asked, "How many days' ride?"

"One long day in good weather. But with two feet of snow and two layers of crust I suspect we should of been out of here yesterday."

Next morning they were on the trail again.

This time it was easy to follow because fence posts lined the route. A couple of hours from the line cabin the wire played out, but the posts still marched straight over the gently rolling ground to lose themselves in the glare of unpolluted snow. By midafternoon there was a subtly different quality to the air and neither Paddy nor the horses were breathing quite so raggedly. Finally he understood that they were still descending and that the gentle, rolling appearance of the country managed to conceal how steeply everything tilted from the customary angle. Back at the cabin the creek had performed a couple of perfunctory meanders. Now it ran straight as the fence posts and had cut a channel so deep that the poplars and willows were invisible a hundred yards away.

"Been wanting to ask," the boy said after an hour of silence. "This Lawson estate—'tis cows you raise?"

"Always figgered that was why they called me a cowboy," Jug said.

"Then why have I seen so few of them?"

"That would make a man ponder," Jug agreed.

Paddy was remembering the last time he had heard that phrase when Ottie added, "The roundup's over. Breeding stock's all down on the lower range till the new grass comes next spring."

"Is that all the country's good for? Can't a man grow anything here?"

"Rattlesnakes maybe—if you have a good wet year."

"Has anybody ever tried?"

"Long as old Bill Lawson's alive, nobody better."

"Who was it started to build a cabin up there in Poplar Fork?"

"'Fore my time."

Paddy thought a moment. "How old is Mr. Lawson?" he finally asked.

"Old enough."

Paddy shrugged and wondered if the news would have reached County Down as yet that his gentleman had passed on. Couldn't, he decided. He had to get to a constable and report what had happened. And then the trouble would start at home. His gentleman had died without issue. But the estate, Paddy knew, was entailed, since They were never much for splitting an inheritance into unlivable fractions. They always entailed, leaving everything to an eldest son, and it was up to the rest of the brood to go out and steal a living as best they could. So now what distant heir from what distant part of the Empire would come to rape the land where Paddy had grown up—where his mother still struggled to survive?

"What happens when Mr. Lawson dies?"

"You don't ever need to worry about that, boy. Old Bill's too tough to die."

"I'm no boy anymore. 'Tis twenty-one I am now."

"Right you are, Pistol. And don't you forget it." Both men seemed to extract more amusement from this than Paddy could find in a simple and necessary exaggeration.

That night they camped down out of the wind in the eroded creekbed. There was still snow on the ground, but down here there was no ice along the edges of the fast-flowing stream. While the men unsaddled and hobbled, Paddy added water to the half-cooked and drained beans he had packed all day. Wood was plentiful but so uniformly wet that finally he used up a candle stub getting the fire started.

"After the first hundred years you'll get to where you like beans," Jug assured him from across the campfire.

Paddy guessed he could get used to anything in a hundred years, but it seemed a long while since he had savored oats or barley or cabbage and praties or any of the things God-fearing people were wont to eat. He cleaned the Peacemaker again and polished a hint of green from the brass cartridge casings, meanwhile covertly studying the two murderers. Several times he almost asked the question that was on his mind, but each time he stopped, knowing it was too dangerous. Since he had been with these men Paddy had struggled to play the boy: fey, feckless, and forgetful. But even though he was now twenty-one, the boy could remember when he had been sixteen. It seemed like only yesterday. He polished the pistol and waited.

Next day at noon he saw the headquarters of the Bar L. He wondered what he had been expecting. Surely not the baronial splendor of Himself's estate, with its centuries-old buildings and their eternal fires to fend off the rising damp. The Lawson estate was a cluster of pole corrals and deal sheds which, on closer inspection, turned out not to be of sawn boards but of squared-off logs chinked with some kind of white clay or mortar.

The boy recognized stables and a smithy. There were

barns and storerooms of various kinds, and his rescuers, after corraling their horses, led him to a long, barrackslike building, which turned out to be precisely that. "Gitcherself cleaned up a little," Jug said, and left him half a bar of soap and a bucket warming on the bunkhouse stove. Both men disappeared.

Was this really the seat of the estate? He had seen nothing that even remotely suggested a great house. Nor was there anyone in the bunkhouse he could ask. Most bunks had blankets, though, and there was personal gear strewn about the room. He removed his tattered tweeds and began scrubbing loose two months' worth of grime and dead skin. As he put his only clothes back on, even Paddy was nearly overcome by the wet-dog stink of sheep. He was cleaning the Peacemaker when Jug and Ottie returned.

"Leave that thing behind if you want to keep it," Ottie warned.

"Where we goin'?"

"*We* done been already. Now it's your turn. And if you want to get along in this country, remember you got to get along with old Bill."

Paddy's life had been spent getting along with two of the most capricious and flighty species of unintelligence in Ireland. He had been only fifteen when last he curried the favor of one and the hide of the other. As Ottie led him past the corral to a smaller and less pretentious building, he remembered the day his father had outfitted him in the family best and taken him up to the great house to be inspected. The ceremony had not been too different from the way the boy had learned to lead horses and display their gaits to prospective buyers.

Eight or ten men already waited in line before the building. Paddy had no wish to appear simple before strangers, so he asked no questions. Ottie traded jokes and news with the others until it was his turn to go in. So what was it? Paddy wondered if it was the custom of this country for everyone to undergo a soul-searching and rehiring every new year.

But these men were all cheerful and none seemed worried at any prospect of losing his post. Minutes passed and Ottie came out. He pushed the boy through the door with a grin and a gesture that probably meant good luck.

Paddy stood blinking. There was a sheet-iron stove glowing in one corner, but the only other light came from a tiny window in the opposite side of the room. It was a moment before he could see that a chair and homemade desk had been placed to extract the maximum from that light. The man at the desk was old enough. He was clean-shaven, which, for Paddy, was novel in this land of the unshorn. The owner of the Bar L wore pince-nez spectacles and squinted furiously as he struggled with a ledger. Without looking up he made a shushing gesture and continued mumbling to himself.

The boy had not the foggiest idea what these rituals meant, but he had learned not to interrupt the steward of Himself's estate until that acolyte of accounting saw fit to return to the realm of the unenlightened.

Was this really the old Bill Lawson, who held the whole country in awed thralldom? He was not a particularly large man. Paddy had been expecting an ogre complete with horns and forked tail. He reminded himself that what gentry he had dealt with in the Old Country had often seemed as inoffensive as this until they opened their mouths. But back there at least a gentleman dressed his part. This old man wore the same tight blue canvas trousers with copper-riveted pockets, the same flannel shirt and venerable waistcoat as all the other men on the estate.

He made that shushing gesture again and Paddy abruptly realized the old man meant for him to sit down. He was still trying to digest the strange customs of this egalitarian dictatorship when the old man finally looked up. "What do you want?" Lawson demanded.

Later, when he had time to think about it, the boy wondered if it was his unexpected promotion from sixteen to twenty-one that influenced his reply. Probably not. Mainly, he was remembering the old Scotsman who had taken him in, had treated him like one of God's creatures, taught him to shoot. He wondered if there was the slightest chance that the old shepherd might have survived—lit out in a different direction and gone home to enjoy those six pounds a month or whatever he had been putting away. But as the boy studied this irascible old bastard there was little doubt in his mind who would answer for the Scotsman, for the sheep, for all the hell Paddy had endured getting down out of the mountains. This bald-headed bastard was no better than an Indian. And a name like Lawson just had to be English.

"Speak up, boy. What the hell's your name?"

"Padraig Ó Súilleabháin," the boy said. "And 'tis nothin' I'd be wantin' from the likes of you." As he said it Paddy realized it was not the best opening for getting along with old Bill Lawson. But at least he had the undivided attention of those glacial eyes.

Chapter 10

Lawson's stare was unblinking as an eagle's and with somewhat less of any human quality. It lasted until the boy nearly surrendered into mumblings and explanations but he was sustained by the finely honed grudge that had gone unavenged through all the years from sixteen to twenty-one. The old man spoke first. "So you're the one," he growled. "Why'd you kill Brutus?"

Paddy had been half expecting the question. "If it's reasons you're wantin', you can start with the shot he put at me and me wid no gun and findin' a stranger pilferin' me pack."

There was a hint of surprise. "So you *did* kill him?"

"If it's reasons you're wantin', 'tis tired I am o' bein' called 'boy.' I grew up the day I buried my gentleman and bad cess to his memory, but he was *my* gentleman and the day will come when that lumpy-jawed savage pays me his due. And no, I'd not see me soul in hell for the likes of your blackamoor. 'Tis himself he put down."

"Lump jaw?"

"I'm wishin' it on every cow you'll ever hope to get!" Then he realized the old man was asking about the Indian and not about the nodes that are equally incurable on man and cow. "Ah then you'll be knowin' who he is and you'll not be tryin' to tell me there's no Indians in this country?"

"Of course there are Indians. Now why would Brutus kill himself?"

"Might be for havin' no foot. Or it might be his conscience was so clean he'd take his chances on heaven instead of another winter here."

"And is your conscience that good?"

The boy thought a moment. "This world is filled with them as did evil to me and mine. And I've not killed one of them yet. Nor have I killed those who did me no harm. 'Tis me own failin' I must confess. Give me some time about the likes o' you and I'll get the hang of it."

"You'll hang all right," Lawson said musingly. He twisted in his chair and rubbed his nose where the pince-nez had dug in. "So you've no need of me. And what're your plans from here on, boy?"

"'Tis no boy I am and in this country 'tis no use making plans."

Lawson studied him for another expressionless minute. "Well, I don't need you any more than you need me." Paddy was turning when the old man sighed and added, "But they tell me you know horses. If you want to stay on it's thirty a month. Beans and cartridges free."

Paddy weighed two hundred unhorsed miles against the condition of his boots. "Thirty what?"

For an instant there was almost amusement in those glacial eyes. "Dollars. They run about five to the pound," he explained. He turned the ledger around to face the boy. "Can you write your name?"

"Irish, English, or Latin?"

Once more a hint of surprise. Paddy saw no point in adding that, apart from this triplicate feat cribbed from a baptismal certificate, he knew little else of writing. He seized the pen and tried not to stick out his tongue as he chiseled Padraig Ó Súilleabháin. But there was no end of odd ways in this country. In Ireland his gentleman had merely grunted the boy into a lifetime of stables. Here Lawson thrust page after page of printed forms at him and patiently showed the boy where to wrestle with the scratchy steel nib. Finally there were no more sheets of foolscap to sign.

"You'll need clothes and a saddle," Lawson grunted. "That'll just about wipe out your wages to date."

Easy come, easy go. Paddy hadn't known he was on the payroll.

"Send Ottie back in here."

Paddy did. A moment later Ottie emerged with a key in hand and moments after that the boy emerged from the store with one each of Levi's and everything else, including high-heeled boots. Ottie helped by carrying the new saddle and used bridle back to the bunkhouse.

Paddy stuffed his tweeds into the bunkhouse stove and spent the rest of the day repenting as he struggled to rearrange his private parts within the confines of new Levi's. He worked saddle soap into the odd wood and leather contraption that people in this country insisted was a saddle, and wondered why his brand-new blazer would have an unsewn pocket that let his hand through into the endless expanse of coat lining. But mostly he spent the day wondering why the master of this rustic estate had not shot him, hanged him, or sent him packing.

Throughout the afternoon other men arrived chilled and windburned on horses whose steaming breath reminded Paddy of a chromo of St. George and the dragon. He laid claim to an upper bunk before all the empty spaces disappeared. The bunk was as innocent of springs as the loft where Paddy had slept at home. He wondered at the greenish dust in the straw tick and was on the point of tasting it when a stranger slapped his hand down. "That's Paris green, boy! You may be crazier'n a bedbug but they ain't no point in endin' up dead."

There was a sudden and infernal racket outside and abruptly men were stampeding from the bunkhouse. But there were so many riders converging on the ranch that by the time Paddy had gotten outside the cook had stopped jangling his triangle so the boy had to await a second sitting. Supper was not much of a meal to his way of thinking, but the stew had a few carrots and turnips with the potatoes and was a welcome change from the line cabin's beans and biscuits. He had learned to endure coffee by now, but it never failed to amaze him the way these ravenous men gulped it with never a longing word for a nice cuppa tea. He was about to ask the cook if he had any when he noticed that man's speculative look at the youngest man at the long table. Paddy finished eating and made tracks before he could be drafted into dishwashing.

Every spare bit of floor in the bunkhouse was occupied and still men were arriving. New Year's must be quite an affair in this country. But why the air of gloating conspiracy among all these windburned riders?

Paddy had seen this furtive holiday air before—usually when he accompanied his father and had a glass of small beer while men held hushed conversations and shook hands. It was not until he had been older that Paddy noted how these meetings often occurred only hours before the shooting of some particularly obnoxious landlord. He cornered Jug. "What's on for tomorrow?"

"You'll see."

The last time these ruffians had sallied out to kill sheep, Paddy had been on the other end of it. He suspected he was not going to like this side any better.

It was still bitter cold next morning but the wind had died when forty men rode out from the Bar L with old Bill Lawson at their head. It struck Paddy as particularly ironic that men who could not abide sheep all wore woolen underwear and shirts, and half of them were in sheepskin blazers. But he was having his own problems getting used to a saddle that was different from anything he had ever ridden, and a pair of trousers that kept forcing things into the wrong places. He saw Jug and Ottie and spurred his roan—a skittish beast that did not seem properly broken to the bit—until they rode abreast. "Where we goin'?" Paddy repeated.

"Town."

"Two hundred miles?"

Both riders stared. "What gave you that idea?"

"Your black friend."

Ottie shook his head sadly. "Brutus was gettin' along, all right."

Paddy was not sure what this meant. "He had all his wits about him the last time we talked."

"Oh he was all right," Jug said. "But you got to remember *old* Brutus went off to the war to take care of *young* Mr. Lawson."

Paddy, whose people supplied cannon fodder for the endless wars of Empire, had no idea which war they meant. But if Brutus had been old when the old man at the head of this column was young . . . he remembered the black man's grizzling hair. "So how far is it to the nearest town?"

"Another two or three hours." Jug screwed up his forehead. "Town's only been here a couple of years. Brutus, now he was pretty much like old Bill. One of them don't like somethin', he's liable to go on thinkin' it just ain't there."

Considering that Lawson was leading this column to town, Paddy was hard pressed to see the logic in Jug's explanation. "Himself didn't want the town?"

"Towns mean people. People's just like sheep."

Paddy had heard priests talk of flocks and the Lamb of God. He could not fit the analogies to the matter at hand.

"Sheep eat grass," Ottie explained. "And people plow it under."

Suddenly Paddy was very aware of the Peacemaker pounding his thigh with each jolt of the trotting roan. "How many people in this town?"

"Twenty. Maybe thirty."

And forty riders coming in from the Bar L! "Is there hope they'll be clearin' out before we get there?"

Jug laughed. "Ruby's the county seat these days. Sheriff and all them taxpayers don't scare for sour owl puke. Took a while, but now even old Bill knows land and money can only do so much."

To Paddy it had always seemed as if this combination was only slightly less omnipotent than the wrath of God.

"Money can buy a few votes," his mentor explained. "But

you git storekeepers and preachers and sodbusters overrunnin' the country and joinin' granges and organizin' . . . Legislature may not know right from wrong but them shypokes know how to sniff out a vote. Just ain't that easy no more for an old man to hang onto all the land he run the Indians off of."

"What Indians?"

"Oh they used to be some bad ones. They're starvin' up around Fort Rudge now while the beef ring gets rich. Seems like everybody makes money off a cow 'cept the man raises it."

All of which told the boy nothing about the Indians he didn't already know. He tried a different tack. "I don't know that much about cows. Himself seemed to think I was goin' to look after horses."

But Jug was from a country where people mean what they say and he was totally unused to this oblique Irish way of leading up to important matters. "What the hell you talkin' about?"

"Earnin' me keep! If I was never fool enough to take the Queen's shilling and go kill fuzzie-wuzzies, then why should it be worth six pounds for me to kill Protestants?"

"Plumb loco." Then Jug's eyes narrowed in understanding. "You think we're goin' in to shoot up the town?" He laughed. "Hell, boy, this is eighteen and eighty-one. Times is civilized."

"Then why's every man jack in this column carryin' a gun?"

"Well," Ottie said, "I wouldn't want to trust civilization too far."

Drafted! Somebody else's army, somebody else's war, and 'tis not even the right side I'm on. He checked the pistol and wished there'd been more ammunition at the line cabin, and better weather so he could have stayed outside long enough to learn how to use it. He had spent hours drawing and snapping the empty Peacemaker while Ottie and Jug were out stretching barbed wire but they had warned him that a shot would bring them back both loaded for bear, so he still did not know how the heavy weapon would react with live ammunition.

What he did know was that Ottie and Jug must have been in on the raid that killed the Scotsman and the sheep, almost killed Paddy. Still, he found it hard to sustain his hate against these simple men who treated him no worse than had the Scotsman—and with more unpremeditated kindness than he had ever experienced from his gentleman. Even Lawson, who rode bundled in a sheepskin coat at the head of the column . . . The old spalpeen had treated Paddy better than the boy's abrasive approach had deserved. Bucko or not, the old man seemed to have no difficulty commanding the loyalty of these men.

What did Paddy really know about this country and its feuds? Lawson was trying to hang onto his own. Wouldn't any man? If he were to apply strict logic, Paddy would find himself allied with the Indians old Lawson had evicted, who had amused themselves poking holes in Paddy's tender hide. As he remembered the way that most especially accursed pagan with all the bad teeth in a lumpy jaw had prodded and driven him away from the trail to Fort Rudge, Paddy's hand drifted to caress the butt of the Peacemaker. Someday he would find that savage again.

But even the most fine-honed hatred can know moments of lapse on a morning not all that bad, with new clothes and a new saddle and a full stomach. The Bar L riders accepted the boy. For the first time in his life he was a man. He had a gun and he was riding with this band of brothers. It was a new land with new opportunities. Maybe he should forget old hatreds and old ties. He hadn't volunteered to come here. His gentleman had taken him. He felt a slight qualm about the old Scotsman—and none at all for the absentee owner of those sheep. The old herder had warned him: If you don't turn hard, you're not long for it.

But each time he had nearly convinced himself, Paddy remembered these—some of these men, anyway—were the same who had poured bullets into his camp, never once asking if he cared to become involved in local problems.

He was on the wrong side. Maybe every side was wrong. He knew horses but he didn't belong here. He didn't know sheep. He didn't want to know any more Indians. Perhaps, as the Scotsman had pointed out, the antelope and buffalo had the only legitimate claim.

If only it could be as simple as it had been back home, where the choice was a simple us or Them, with no holds barred and no vitiating ability to see the other side of the argument . . .

He had dropped behind Jug and Ottie and now rode abreast of a young man whose hair was red as Paddy's, and who couldn't be that much older. They might have been friends—if he could believe this young redhead had never shot at him, forced him to walk his boots off, freeze, and starve.

Get away from this mob of freebooters. Warn the town? Devil take them! Probably just as bad as this lot. Paddy inventoried his condition. He didn't have any money but he had new clothes, a horse, and a saddle. He had a pistol. Nobody was paying him any real attention. All he had to do was fall back slowly to the rear of the column. Once there he could stop long enough to tighten a cinch or pick a stone from his mount's frog and once the last man was out of sight Paddy would be on his way: two hundred miles downstream, downhill to civilization. Let them all kill one another!

Then as he looked up, Paddy knew it was too late. They were already nearing the county seat of Ruby.

Chapter 11

At least he supposed it was the town. They topped a slight rise and below lay a cluster of shacks and false fronts bisected by a yellow line where the snow had been tinted with the by-products of horse-drawn civilization. Though it was a relatively fine day, this was still not the kind of weather that brought whittlers out on the front stoop. The forty riders made another half mile and Paddy could see the town clearly when a man stepped from a building to pick his way through frozen muck and offal toward the other side of the single street. He saw the approaching column. As he sprinted the rest of the way across Paddy knew any slight hope of surprise was gone.

He waited for old Lawson to signal the column out into line-of-skirmishers but nothing happened. Paddy had never been a soldier but every old man in Ireland had. The boy had listened to tactics and revolution all his life. In a minute the townspeople would start shooting and with the column bunched up this way . . .

He wanted to pull up lame and let the rest of these fools take the first volley, but it was too late now. Fall back and the man behind would encourage his horse with a rope end.

Paddy's life had been innocent of all those fairy tales about the carefree gallantry of Irish troops. Instead, he had been steeped in the other side of soldiering—armless, legless, eyeless remnants of men who metered their whiskey against their twinges and endlessly reminisced glory-hunting commanders who, untainted with any Irish blood, felt no compunction about spilling it.

Paddy was appalled. Were these men brave or just stupid? They were older than he. Didn't they know what was going to happen any minute now? How could they indulge in small talk as if they were off on holiday?

And still they rode bunched up in column of twos, past the first house where a woman's pale face showed as she hastily closed the door. Another moment and they would be in the middle of the town, taking fire from all sides. Had any of these New World innocents ever heard of the Light Brigade? Paddy muttered an Act of Contrition and braced himself against the abundance of God's grace to come.

But it didn't come. They rode past public houses whence painted women stared, past the smithy, the mercantile, the surveyor's, and the land office. Curtains twitched and once a woman sallied out to scoop a child away from the advancing column. And still the shooting didn't come.

Despite the chill Paddy was sweating but he was afraid to unbutton his coat lest that innocent gesture precipitate a hail of lead. "Sure a sorry-lookin' bunch, ain't they?" the cheerful young man to his right observed.

Paddy nodded absently. He caught his hand fiddling with the already fraying fringe of the pocket in his new coat and reminded himself to sew it up someday. But right now prudence dictated that his hands be out in plain sight.

The board fronts were plastered with tattering papers. Every second one began with a PUBLIC NOTICE, then dwindled into print too small for the boy even to wonder if he could read it. They continued down the gauntlet of a street and still nobody fired the first shot as Lawson pulled up and hitched before the largest building in town. In front of it stood a knot of men who glowered at the old man's forty pistoleers but did nothing to provoke them. A man with some sort of star-shaped badge on his calfskin vest emerged from a doorway to study them. And still nothing happened!

"They comin'?" the man with the star asked Lawson.

The old man stared for a moment, then came reasonably close to a grin. "Sooner or later," he said. "And when they do, all these sober citizens will be delighted to welcome us."

"Who's comin'?" Paddy whispered.

The young man beside him shrugged. "Indians, I s'pose."

But if the citizens of Ruby would be delighted someday to welcome the Bar L, it was evidently not today. "Then what brings you?" the sheriff demanded. He was an elderly man—not as old as Bill Lawson, but with a weathered, nononsense look to him. "This's a peaceable town. We plan on keepin' it that way."

"Then I can count on your people not to go getting itchy and starting something?" Lawson asked.

"Any shootin' starts you can count on me," the sheriff said flatly. "And they won't be no flapdoodle about who I come looking for. This is my town and those are your men."

Paddy held his breath but Lawson only smiled. "You're living in the past, Sheriff. We didn't come to town for any big New Year's shindy."

The sheriff stood feet apart, not at all intimidated by having to look up to a man on horseback.

"Strictly business," Lawson said, "and I'm counting on you, Sheriff, to see that none of *your* people interfere while mine exercise their lawful rights as citizens."

The sheriff favored Lawson with a sour grin. "You must've lost track of your calendar out there," he said. "There ain't no election today."

"I know," Lawson said, "and I wouldn't dream of interfering in town affairs. After all, we're not legal residents of Ruby; only of the territory." He turned from the sheriff to open a saddlebag. He pulled out a handful of papers and went into the courthouse.

The Bar L men sat their horses. Jug and Ottie took it on themselves to keep some kind of order while Paddy struggled to guess what the hell was going on. The sheriff stood before his office studying the column warily but the boy sensed that the moment for shooting had passed. He oozed his horse up beside Jug and Ottie. "Is this town on Bar L land?" he asked.

Jug frowned and considered. "Depends," he said. "No

white man ever dast come in here till old Bill run the Indians off. Now them sodbusters come in and grab all the water and . . ." He shrugged.

Lawson emerged from the courthouse door long enough to call, "Abraham Abbott and William Brown."

Two men dismounted. Old Bill handed each a fistful of papers and ushered them inside. From across the street townspeople glowered but nobody seemed ready to fire the first shot.

The sheriff stood staring at the Bar L riders but none of the men Paddy rode with made a move for his weapon. They seemed amused—as if some great coup had been pulled off and they had every reason to congratulate themselves.

Paddy couldn't understand it. The town seemed in awe of them. Yet the sheriff had, almost, welcomed them at first, seemed to think they were coming in to establish common cause against the Indians. And would these glowering townspeople also try to tell Paddy there weren't any Indians around here?

"Donald Curtis and Howard Dalton!"

Two more men into the courthouse as the first pair emerged and handed papers to Lawson for safekeeping. As they climbed aboard their horses the Bar L riders raised a faintly derisive cheer. The town men across the street saw nothing funny about it.

Paddy sighed, knowing nobody was going to tell him any more. Here he was in town, in civilization for the first time since his gentleman and Mr. Bridgeman had been murdered. He ought to be telling this sheriff what had happened, but there seemed little chance that he would ever get to exchange anything except bullets with that hard-looking man. He ought to be hunting out a priest and performing the necessary rituals to cleanse his soul, but there was no indication that any of these people were not heathen. And even if he were to see a priest or a church nobody was straying from the waiting column of Bar L men.

How far down the alphabet was Ó Súilleabháin? A bottle appeared and began its way down the column. Just sitting here was not nearly as warm as riding had been. Paddy hoped the bottle would not be empty before it reached him, but at that moment old Lawson saw his men drinking.

"Put it away!" It was a roar worthy of the beast from Revelation. "I'll have no man say there was drunkenness on this day!"

The Bar L riders grumbled but the bottle disappeared before it could do Paddy any good. He twisted in the saddle and grudgingly admitted to himself that this grotesque, high-horned contraption was surprisingly comfortable for all-day sitting, even if it did seem harder on the horses than English pads.

There were public houses here offering warmth and other attractions. Either old Lawson commanded more loyalty than Paddy had thought or perhaps these men did not care to venture singly among the scowling townsfolk. The Bar L men did not dismount, save one at a time to check cinches. Despite their casual appearance Paddy sensed that the trouble was still not over. He studied the layout of the single-street town and tried to select which way he would run when it started.

Gradually it dawned on him that no townsman was on horseback that day. When it happened they would know each other instantly: horse against foot. If he were to make his escape two hundred miles down to the rivermouth or wherever civilization would turn out to be the next time somebody lied to him, Paddy was going to need a good horse. He was also going to need the luck of the storybook Irish who never seemed to suffer famines or death or any of the slings and arrows of English arrogance. Somehow he had to get through this tangle of buildings before he was cut down by one side or the other. And bad cess to both of them!

"Rupert Davis and Herman Eckhardt!"

Time to be gone. Slip away now before it starts and you

can be ten miles down the trail while these ruffians do each other in. But as he studied the glowering sheriff and townsfolk the boy knew it was already too late. If the Bar L riders did not shoot him in the back for desertion, he would still not last a hundred yards alone once he left the protection of that leather-lunged old bastard whose head emerged from the courthouse to call another pair of names. Only this time one name was Paddy's. He left his roan ground-tied and walked forward to accept a handful of papers. He had scarcely time to recognize that they were the same ones he had signed in the old man's office yesterday. Lawson gave a hint of a grin as he led the boy down a hall and pushed him through an open door.

Paddy stood before a balding man who looked as if he had just discovered he was in the wrong line of work. "Well?" the little man snapped.

"I am."

The man behind the desk looked up. "You're what?"

"Well," Paddy replied.

"The papers," the small man said with a heavenward glance.

"Oh." Paddy handed them over.

"Seem to be in order," the man said grudgingly. "Your name's Patrick O'Sullivan?"

"Me mother always said it was."

The little man looked up from the papers. "Says you're an American citizen here. How come you talk like an Irishman?"

"Maybe it's because I am an Irishman."

Before he could add anything more, old Lawson was beside him and smoothly interjected, "Son of Brian Sullivan, veteran of the 4th Volunteers. Now you wouldn't dispute a Union veteran's son's derivative citizenship just because the lad happened to spend a few years in Ireland?"

The registrar decided he would not—at least not while the Bar L was out in force. "Do you hereby solemnly swear the information herein is true, so help you God? Raise your right hand and say 'I do.'"

Paddy was about to say there were no volunteers in Ireland and in any event his father's name had been Gavin and bedamned if he'd be makin' any claims to citizenship in this benighted wilderness when abruptly the force of old Bill Lawson's boot in his ankle and elbow in ribs was enough to elicit a startled grunt.

The registrar accepted this noise as an affirmative. "Poplar Fork," he grunted. "Now where in hell's that?"

"Farthest section on the northern boundary," Lawson said.

Paddy was having misgivings. Was this country at war again? He remembered the story that had made the rounds of the Ould Sod about the young men of a generation ago who had come ashore at Boston or New York and been met by a smooth, Irish-speaking gentleman who offered them well-paying jobs driving the horse cars, with food and new clothes thrown in. These prospective horse-car drivers had not known what they signed and swore to until they discovered they were now in a Protestant army and marching off to murder Catholics. Whole battalions had deserted to reenlist on the Mexican side.

"I'll be doin' no fightin' for no side—" the boy began, but Lawson had already hustled him out of the building and was now calling Robert Wrigley and Hamish Zimmerman.

"So what is it?" he demanded of Jug and Ottie. "Is it a soldier he'll be makin' of me?"

The older men stared a moment, then laughed. "No fightin', boy," Ottie said. "That's for the old days. These sodbusters all believe in doin' things legal and tiein' a man up in papers and red tape. Now us Bar L boys ain't legal residents of Ruby. But we been in the territory since't before this town was ever built, so ain't nobody can say we ain't got a right."

"Right to what? What am I in for?"

"Congratulations," Jug said. "In one week you've aged five years and you're an American citizen."

"Not only that," Ottie grinned, "you're a landowner too. Bet you never thunk in Ireland you was goin' to end up a man of property."

Still Paddy didn't understand.

"Homestead law," Jug explained. "First of the year they opened it up. Them sodbustin' shypokes was gonna grab off every watered section of Bar L. Never happened to think we might do it ourselves. Congratulations again, boy. You're now the owner of one square mile of land up around Poplar Fork."

"Then don't call me 'boy.'"

Chapter 12

Finally every Bar L man had his section: forty square miles of watered land, and if any sodbuster wanted the rest of this dehydrated region he was welcome. Old Lawson had dispatched three men downriver toward the territorial capital with duplicate copies of each declaration—all signed and sealed by an unsmiling registrar, who watched his last opportunity of "losing" these papers go trotting down the trail with three men, three repeating rifles, and three fast horses.

The Bar L riders had hung around town for a couple of hours. Lawson divided them into two watches and sent one group to the nearest saloon to warm up and wet their collective whistle. After one startled look, the local drinkers had suddenly remembered urgent business elsewhere. While one squad warmed up, the other kept an eye on every way out of town lest someone consider interfering with Lawson's insurance against legal error.

Only when the three riders had an unalterable head start had thirty-seven of Lawson's forty men taken the nosebags from their mounts and ridden back toward the ranch. It had been a long, nerve-wracking day, but throughout it all Paddy had not heard a single shot. He wondered how many more days like this he would endure.

"So what's all this about ownin' land?" he pursued.

Ottie tried to screw his neck down deeper into his sheep and denim jacket. "Them sodbusters figger since old Lawson run the Indians off it's only fair they run him off. They passed a new law. All a man has to do is sign the papers and grab his 640 acres and all at once he owns a mile of this territory."

Paddy doubted if his gentleman's estate in Ireland had been much larger. "But don't I have to pay?"

Ottie struggled to get his hat farther down over prominent ears. With snow on the ground and a rising moon there would be no trouble getting home by midnight, but as the sun set the wind rose. "Well," he conceded, "you got to do two things. First, you got to pay two bits an acre."

"Out of my wages, I suppose." Paddy had no idea how much two bits was.

"What the hell, kid, it's less than six months' pay. Anyhow, the hard part's already done."

"Stealin' it from the farmers?"

Ottie grinned and unexpectedly waxed philosophic. "It's a hard world, boy, and a man has to do for himself. If you find a snake in the garden, you're the one that's got to kill it."

"Or an Indian," the boy said thoughtfully.

"The hard part," Ottie repeated. "The Desert Land Act of 1877 is a little different from the other Homestead Acts. You also got to 'create a water supply.'"

Paddy's mind was still on killing snakes and Indians.

"That dam upstream of where you buried old Brutus," the cowboy explained. "We 'created' it years ago before anybody ever thought about puttin' a plow to this country."

"How about that cabin somebody started to build in the Fork?"

"How about it?"

"Who started it?"

Ottie shrugged. "Some pilgrim come in and figured God shoveled up that dam special for him. Lawson warned him plenty of times not to go interferin' between Bar L cattle and Bar L water. Some people just won't listen to reason."

Like Scots sheepherders. "I suppose whoever started that cabin had nothin' to do with arrowheads I found there?"

Ottie gave him an odd look. "Whose side you on, boy?"

"Every side I pick turns out losin'," Paddy said. "I started out bein' born Irish. Then I came to this country to tend me gentleman's horses. And then . . ." He had been about to recount his adventures with the Scots sheepherder when he remembered where he was, and that Ottie had probably been one of those who shot up the camp.

"Well, you can't complain about your luck now, boy. You're fed and got clothes on your back and now you're a landowner."

"What happens if I go live on *my* land and work it my own way?"

"Don't push your luck, boy. I heard you jawin' away at old Bill. Seemed like they could hear you clear into Ruby." The older man struggled to settle deeper into his collar. "You got no cause to jaw an old man that way. 'Specially when he's just learnt his oldest friend is dead. Damn'd if I can understand why he didn't just send you packin'."

It was a question that had been bothering Paddy too. Hints of explanation hovered at the edge of his mind but he didn't like to think about them. "Those arrowheads," he persisted. "How long since any Indians lived there?"

"Lived where?"

"Poplar Fork."

Ottie didn't know. "Ain't no Indians this side of the mountains anymore."

"Funny."

"Not really. Them savages was a bad bunch but by the time the last of them got rounded up they was kind of pitiful. Used to be some rode for the Bar L but they just can't stay away from booze."

That had not been what Paddy meant. He remembered how the sheriff had seemed almost to welcome the Bar L—until he learned an Indian attack was not imminent. "Has our lord and master been spreadin' stories about the wild Indians to keep the townsfolk in their place?"

Ottie's eyes were streaming from the chill wind. He wiped

them with his bandanna and considered the question. "You know," he chuckled, "I wouldn't put it past the old bastard."

Paddy decided he wouldn't either.

But who was the villain in this land of no friends? Indian against white, cow against sheep, farmer against all. The buffalo had lost their claim to grass, but deer and antelope still struggled for theirs—and were left to rot by cowmen and sheepmen who had no notion of sharing.

It was true. Lawson had treated Paddy with more forbearance than a lippy boy deserved. Lawson's claim was better than any of the latecomers' who struggled to displace him. But Paddy's distrust was as instinctual as if the boss of the Bar L had been English.

Damn him, he thought. I didn't ask to be a landowner. Who'd want to live in this Purgatory? Even in his new clothes the boy was feeling the cold now that night fell and the wind rose. The horses bounced along more stiff-legged than usual from the cold, jouncing a little warmth into him, but even with buckskin gloves he had to keep switching reins as he warmed first one hand, then the other inside his jacket. His feet were starting to go numb.

In the dusk he could see several men afoot, jogging beside their horses. Paddy dismounted and endured flaming agony as life returned to his feet. Why in hell were they riding on a night like this?

As if he didn't know! If the Bar L bunch had tried to spend a night in town there would have been trouble. They all knew it. None of these freezing men was complaining. His feet warmed and he got back atop his roan. "'Nother ten miles," Jug said consolingly.

Clouds sailed past the moon but it never became too dark to see the trail. The column clopped on and finally Paddy was stripping tack from his horse, strapping on a blanket before he slapped it into the Bar L corral. The collie pranced up to greet him.

There was hot soup and bread and slabs of smoking steak. Men ate in weary silence, then filtered quietly back to the bunkhouse. There was a strange bindle in Paddy's bunk. His own blankets were tossed onto the floor. He put the bindle on the floor and remade his bunk. The collie came in and scooted quietly underneath the bunk. Paddy was sliding into his blankets when the owner of the bindle came in. He looked at his roll of blankets and at Paddy. Paddy looked back.

The other man was approaching middle age and had the red-rimmed eyes and sour look of the world's losers. "That's my bunk," he growled.

"It wasn't last night." Paddy turned to the other suddenly silent men. "Is there a man here will tell me it's his?"

There was not.

"Then this place is mine."

The other shifted his attack. "And, boy, you git that goddamn stinkin' dog out of here!" he snarled.

"'Tis not the dog whose stink I'm smellin'."

The red-eyed man gave an inarticulate roar and charged before Paddy was totally free of entangling blankets. The boy managed to divert his charge to one side while he freed himself. The next time the man charged he launched a savage attack with his nose against Paddy's fist. While his eyes were uncrossing the boy got a blanket over the other man's head. One twist and the man was helpless.

"I'm not used to your ways," the boy told the circle of grinning cowboys. "Is it with guns, boots, or me fists that I'm to settle this?"

"Why don't you ask him?" a cowboy laughed.

Paddy punched the blanket until he had captured its inhabitant's attention. He repeated the question. The only reply was a muffled roar. The boy sighed and stepped back while the other man disentangled himself. "Will it be guns, boots, or fists?" he repeated.

The man with the red-rimmed eyes abruptly realized he was looking *up* at this clumsy-looking boy. "I'm waitin'," Paddy said.

"You ain't heard the last of this," the stranger snarled, but he wasted no time picking up his bindle.

"Nor have you," Paddy promised. "And unless you're wantin' to settle it now ye'd best keep to the far end of this barrack. But wait along a minute for me to have one good look at the face I'll be rememberin' if anything ever happens to me dog."

Paddy didn't know what was the usual end of these affairs. Every man in the bunkhouse had at least one pistol. Was it like soldiering, where there were unwritten inhibitions against using weapons of war against a fellow soldier? He wondered if congratulations or commiserations were in order. Ottie and Jug seemed to be missing. All he got from the other residents of the bunkhouse was an awed silence.

The lamp was blown out and immediately there was a chorus of snores from exhausted men. Paddy was younger and tireder than they but he could not sleep. Instead, he fought the bout a dozen different ways, wondering if he could have avoided it, if he should have kept on until the other man was pounded beyond rancor and retaliation. What was the custom of this country? Would they hang him for killing a stranger who attacked him? Was there any law at all? Maybe that red-eyed spalpeen was sneaking up on him right now, taking advantage of the dark. If Paddy were to turn up with his throat cut tomorrow what would they do to the other man? He didn't even know his attacker's name.

Where were Jug and Ottie? Where were the two men had dragged him into this, had supposedly befriended him? Where was anybody in his life when he needed him? He felt a slight nudge and nearly yelled before he realized it was only Dorrga's cold nose edging up from under the bunk. He put his hand out and patted the dog back to sleep.

It was dangerous to make enemies. But what else could he have done? The boy had been around enough barnyards to understand what, a century later, would come to be known as pecking order. If he didn't make his position with fists, blade, or bullet there would be no way life could be endured among these murderers. *'Tis a cruel world, lad. If ye dinna' learn that ye're no' long for it.*

Some of those slept under this roof had killed the old man who had given him that bit of advice. The old sheepman had treated him like a human being, had fed him, had taught him to shoot. Somebody had to pay for his death.

But meanwhile Paddy had to survive. Was it their custom to congratulate a winner? Did they gang up like dogs to kill a loser? All he had gotten was an awed silence. If he could not win love Paddy guessed he would settle for respect.

And still he could not sleep. The late supper turned to acid and gouged runnels of fire in his innards as he went over the fight once more. What could he have done differently? If he'd let the red-eyed stranger have the bunk Paddy knew he would end up with nothing. He would live on castoffs, do the jobs nobody else wanted, be last at the table and the first to wash dishes. This was the one-legged future Brutus had foreseen. No wonder the black man had preferred to die.

Paddy decided his instincts had been correct. Fight.

If he had it to do over again there was only one thing he would have done differently: He would have warned the assembled crowd, "Don't ever call me 'boy.'"

And thus, finally, the boy slept.

Chapter 13

Next morning the red-eyed man with matching nose kept to his end of the long table in the cookhouse. After breakfast most of the men made up their bindles and rode off to line cabins, leaving scarcely a dozen hands at the home place. Jug and Ottie were among those who departed. When his enemy failed to appear for dinner, which was what these people called lunch, Paddy supposed he had departed too.

The men who stayed repaired harness and saddles, replaced poles where horses had chewed through the corrals, and did the other chores there would be no time for once grass and spring calving burst upon them.

Paddy looked for a steward but everyone seemed to know his job. Perhaps Lawson ran things himself. But there was no sign of the old man this morning, and Paddy was damned if he would seek him out. He went to the smithy, but a lame elderly man was already presiding over the forge.

"I'm supposed to be a groom," he said. "Would you be knowin' how I'd go about makin' meself useful?"

"Groom?" The farrier laughed. "Ain't no women 'round here. Who you 'spectin' to marry?"

"A *horse* groom," Paddy said patiently.

"You mean a wrangler?"

Paddy guessed he did.

"Well, out there in the corral's some pretty sorry-lookin' nags. Had us a butcher here didn't know which way to point a nail. Don't reckon the horses'll miss him."

"Was he sacked?"

The farrier squinted at the boy. "If that means, 'Did he get kilt?' you done hit it."

Paddy could guess exactly where and when the ex-farrier had died. Who would have believed the old Scotsman could reload a Tower musket that fast? The boy found medicines and spent the rest of the day pine-tarring sore hooves. The farrier finally came out to lean on the corral fence. "They ever kick you?" the graying man asked.

Paddy shook his head. "But often," he conceded, "they kick the place I just vacated."

"Do you have horses like this in Ireland?"

The boy shook his head again. "These are ponies. Our hunters are always at least seventeen hands." He paused to consider. "But I suppose these are tough and take the cold better."

The farrier gave him an odd look. "How long you been in this country?"

It had been nearing September when he and his gentleman sailed from Holywood, which is a short walk downriver from Belfast. It had taken somewhere between a month and a retching eternity to reach Boston. And then there had been an interminable sooty-eyed ordeal on the steam cars.

"You've never spent a summer here?"

Paddy had not.

"You'll find it isn't the cold that's hell on horses or men," the old man said balefully. He stepped into the corral to inspect Paddy's doctoring. "Seem to know your job. Think you can do anything for the sick ones?"

"The what?"

"'Nother corral up at the fort."

"Fort Rudge?" Paddy began to wonder if they were speaking the same language.

The farrier shook his head. "Rudge's way over on the other side of the mountains. Where they got all the Indians corraled." When Paddy remained mystified the old man added, "Fort I'm talkin' about's just the place Lawson holed up his first winter here. Country got a little safer and then he put up the main spread down here where water and grass is handier."

Paddy was wondering if this was why he had not seen the old man since they returned from Ruby when the farrier volunteered, "Gittin' old, I guess. Lately he keeps goin' off there alone. Danged if I can figger what he expects to find. Sure as hell ain't no fountain of youth up that branch."

Paddy had done everything there was to do for the horses here. "Sick ones up there?" he asked.

"Glanders or somethin' catchin'," the farrier said. "Old Bill's mighty particular about anybody goin' back and forth, bringin' it down to this string. Any animal don't look too good, he takes him up there. Ain't never none come back."

Paddy could well believe it if there was glanders among the horses. Throughout his life he had heard rumors of cures. But only rumors. Any man knew the only way to cure glanders was to kill the horse, bury him deep, burn his tack, and scrub the stable—give his leftover feed to the cattle but never to another horse. He was wondering if there might be a different, less virulent form of the disease in this country when the cook's triangle began its unmelodious blather.

So next morning when he could find absolutely no more excuses for hanging around doing nothing he put medicines in saddlebags and picked the oldest, most decayed-looking horse in the corral to ride eight miles up to "You can't miss it; just follow the watercourse."

The weather was still below freezing but the wind was not peeling flesh from bone the way it had the night they rode home from Ruby. He encouraged the aged mare and tried to make Dorrga stay behind but the dog seemed to know something Paddy didn't. He resisted all blandishments until finally the boy gave up and allowed the collie to follow. The trail was half broken and the mare picked her patient way through the crust, stopping occasionally to blow great jets of steam at the collie, who frisked impatiently. In something more than an hour they came onto the "fort."

It was a single square building beside a pole corral. At

first Paddy thought it was of some native stone; then he saw the building had been piled up out of neatly cut blocks of turf. Lodgepole rafters were perilously swayback under the weight of a sod roof. A rusting length of stovepipe thrust through the snow-covered roof. From it came a tendril of white smoke.

So this was where old Lawson hung out. Old men often tired of the company of other generations and preferred their own. Paddy wondered if someday he might come to have nothing in common with those who had not shared the disasters of the years when he had been young. To hell with the old scoundrel. He wanted to be alone, so Paddy would leave him alone. Paddy tied his mare to a scrub pine some distance from the corral and walked over to inspect the sick horses. The dog sniffed and growled.

They didn't look all that sick. More importantly, there was no smell of sickness here. Maybe old Lawson had already culled out those who would die anyway and was waiting like any man with horse sense—not tormenting his beasts with poultices and drenches but just treating them with kindness and waiting to see if God wished them to live.

There were nineteen horses in the corral and a great deal of tack—mostly packsaddles hung from pegs beneath the eaves of the blockhouse. Paddy wondered at the trail that continued on past the corral and up into the mountains. The snow was brown from fresh mud and manure. He put it from his mind to concentrate on the horses. The collie was uninterested in horses but something about this place made him nervous.

There was no hint of glanders among the horses, nor could Paddy see any signs of dourine or any other contagious disease. The horses were thin despite abundant hay in the corral, and their hooves were in bad shape. Two geldings had raw sores on their backs. The boy got out his medicines and went to work.

Jesus, Mary, and Joseph, would his hands ever be warm in this miserable country? He thrust them into the pockets of his mackinaw and bedad if he still hadn't gotten to sewing up that bottomless pocket!

He had cleaned and dusted the geldings' sore backs and was coaxing a mare to lift her foot when the door of the blockhouse burst open. "Who the hell are you and what're you doing here?" Lawson stood in the doorway, a hint of madness in his pale blue eyes, his white hair pointing in every direction. But the shotgun pointed unwaveringly at Paddy.

Paddy's back was hurting from so much straining to lift reluctant horses' hooves. His feet and hands were numb from the cold, and his nose had turned into a fountain. At that moment the mare shifted her hoof and came down squarely on his half-frozen toes.

Paddy's roar was louder than the old man's. "Is it blind y'are too? Who in hell would you think it is? Ye took me on for a groom and 'tis a groom ye got and bad cess to any man'd let his harses go to hell like this!"

The muzzle of the shotgun wavered momentarily but still remained on Paddy. The old man squinted and Paddy abruptly realized that he was at least partially blind. Still pointing the double-barreled twelve-gauge, the old man worked his face as he struggled to see. Dorrga emitted a barely audible growl.

"Ye don't remember me?" Paddy demanded. "Don't remember the owner of a square mile of Poplar Fork?"

"Yes, boy, I know who you are," Lawson said tiredly. "Come in now and sit down for a spell out of the cold."

"I'll be with you when I finish with this mare." The boy turned his back on the shotgun. He had nearly finished all that could be done for these horses, so he doctored another pair of hooves and decided to call it a day before taking up the old man's invitation. There was something odd about the place. Paddy could smell it too—a strange, sweaty, smoky something. The dog didn't like it.

When he finally opened the door to the blockhouse old Lawson had soap and a pan of water warming on the tin stove. Once the boy had rinsed off the inevitable results of handling hooves in a crowded corral he sat to this country's invariable cup of bitter coffee.

"Who told you to come up here?" the old man asked.

"Nobody."

"So why did you come?"

"You took me on for a groom. I've done all that man can do for your beasts down below. And I see no glanders here. Now what would ye have me do?"

Later, on the road back down, Paddy would decide that Lawson must have been devoting some thought to this question while the boy finished up with the horses, for the old man's answer was suspiciously prompt. "Isn't much to do around a ranch this time of year," he said. "And you've worked yourself out of a job even sooner than I'd expected. You're young, boy. And don't go sayin' you're twenty-one. Question is, are you old enough to spend a winter alone?"

"Here?"

Lawson shook his head. "You filed on Poplar Fork. It's time somebody put up a cabin there. Can you do it?"

"I'll need somethin' besides me clasp knife."

Lawson seemed oddly relieved. "Take whatever you need. Farrier can show you where the axes and saws are. But you'd best be on your way if you want to get back before it turns dark."

It was only noon and it had taken Paddy less than an hour to ride up here. But he had learned long ago not to argue with old men. Lawson put on a coat and went outside to help the boy gather up his tools and medicines. He gave the collie an odd look, which Dorrga returned with a hint of a growl. And before Paddy quite realized it he was once more on the ancient mare and riding back down the eight miles to the home ranch. Lawson's parting words had been, "If you need a hand with anything, call on Jug and Ottie. They'll be at the next cabin down."

Paddy spent the afternoon getting kit together for a winter alone. The cook relieved the boy of one worry. "Been puttin' grubstakes together for line cabins longer'n you been alive, boy. I won't forget anything."

In the end the boy decided he would take three horses. If pickings were too slim up at Poplar Fork he could leave one with Jug and Ottie. But would he ever be finished traveling?

He had a proper outfit now—was better dressed than when he had traveled with his gentleman, and it seemed to the boy that it had been centuries ago that he had buried his gentleman and Mr. Bridgeman and been chased by a lumpy-jawed Indian. Since then he had been constantly on the move. Maybe once he had gotten up a roof at Poplar Fork there would be time to sit and digest all the things that had happened.

Landowner . . . now who would have ever thought a groom, son of grooms, would end up a squireen with a whole mile of land? Even in this wilderness 640 watered acres must have some value. But what good was it to him? His land, Paddy suspected, was like his rights in Ireland, where the British, with majestic impartiality, forbade both the rich and the poor to sleep under bridges. "So now I'm a citizen," he told the collie. "Will I be votin' in a free election for whoever it is Themselves see fit to run?"

But Dorrga was uninterested in politics. Paddy checked his supplies once more before going to spend a final night in the bunkhouse. Tomorrow would be a long day and still longer before he would spend another night under a roof. Had he remembered files for saw and ax? Ought to be sleeping but he couldn't. No matter how careful, he knew he would forget something. Ammunition for the Peacemaker? Ought to get a rifle, but there were none laying around unclaimed, and the keys to the store were with old Lawson. He shrugged. Wouldn't be hunting to live anyway. Cookie had assured him there was plenty of jerky in the pack. What was he forgetting?

Endlessly, he ran over mental lists. Salt, soda, flour—cook would have taken care of that. Blankets, matches, candles, tarp . . .

That old scoundrel had acted half crazy when he came storming out with a shotgun. What was wrong with Lawson? So many enemies he was coming to believe everyone was out to do him dirt? But hadn't the old spalpeen ever hauled in his horns when Paddy stood up to him! Almost as if he had been afraid of the boy.

Did the old man have something on his conscience? Something, Paddy amended, apart from the murder of a Scotsman who must have been near as old as Lawson, and the willful destruction of all those sheep? Or could Lawson be remembering after all these years that whoever started that cabin at Poplar Fork must have been a human being too?

It was beyond Paddy. He ran through his lists again, knowing he had covered everything and knowing with equal certainty that once he was too far to turn back he would have turned out to have left his head behind. He was almost asleep when he realized that it was not his list that was bothering him.

Lawson's horses were not diseased. But they had been hard used in the past few days. And the old man had been in a most unholy hurry to see Paddy well away from that fort!

Chapter 14

The sudden realization brought Paddy sitting up in the dark. Dorrga's nose emerged from under the bunk to touch his hand. Lawson had been itching to be rid of him. Lawson had been taking horses up to the fort for reasons he must not want his hands down here to know about. Lawson had been ready to kill him. Would have, the boy decided, if a mare's hoof had not brought such a burst of ferocity from the boy that it had put the old man off just long enough for the moment to pass.

Now what could an evil old man be up to out there in the wilderness? What could he be doing that was so dastardly it must be kept secret even from this band of murderers? Ireland was full of whispered accounts of them as would sell their souls to the powers of darkness. He had never wanted to believe such things, yet he could not ignore the daily evidence of the English who led scandalous lives, reaping where they had not sown, and planting their seed in other men's wives. Could old Lawson have a girl out there?

The boy almost laughed. No matter what dark secret the old man lived with, it would not be that. There was no slightest sign of woman about the blockhouse, and Paddy had lived enough in stables to know the smells of humanity with the same acuity as if he were a horse himself. Had there been a woman there he would know. There had been nothing about the sod fort except the sour goat stink of an old man alone.

He was sure.

Except for that other odd sweet-smoke-sweat stench. Was it rotting harness? The boy slipped from his bunk and into his clothes. Dorrga followed him outside, where the boy sat on the bunkhouse step to put on his boots. It was bitter cold but they were still in the light of the moon. He cautioned the dog with the gesture the Scotsman had used for silence. If only the horses would obey it too. But for once fortune smiled on the boy. He abstracted a mount from the corral and saddled it without arousing anyone. Minutes later he was riding the eight frigid moonlit miles back up toward the fort. "And you keep quiet," he warned the collie.

Bright moonlight reflected off the snow and there was no problem seeing. Having assured himself that there was no disease at the fort, this time Paddy had picked a better horse. He rode at a fast lope, watching steam jet from himself, his mount, and the dog who ranged ahead—but not too far ahead lest he be ganged up on by coyotes who performed noisy rites in obeisance to the full moon.

It was hard to tell time here for, though it was much colder, Paddy had decided he was not as far north as County Down where, in winter, the sun was down by midafternoon and seldom up before time for his elevenses. But it must still be hours short of midnight. The coyotes were suddenly distracted and their hymn to the moon subsided. He saw the outlines of the pole corral and sod house ahead.

Paddy considered tying the horse back where he had tied his mare this morning. But he might want out of here quicker than he had gotten in. Besides, he reasoned, with nineteen horses in the corral, what difference could the sound of one more make? He signaled Dorrga to stay behind and be quiet.

What did he expect to find? The boy didn't have the slightest idea. The night was clear and cold, without the slightest whisper of breeze. Once more he caught a whiff of that odd sweetish stench that seemed equal parts of smoke and sweat.

There were smells, the boy was beginning to realize, that were the signature of every country. It seemed centuries since he had sniffed burning turf with its peat-smoke essence of Ireland. Since then he had spent an eternity in the Purgatory of a steerage passage: fishy salt air and tar, sour vomit, and unwashed child.

Boston: fish and soft coal smoke. He had not been free of coal until they left the steam cars and began traveling with Mr. Bridgeman. The first few days in level untimbered country he had kindled hot, nearly smokeless fires of dried cow dung that smelled not all that different from the turf fires of County Down.

Then they had moved up into the foothills and cooked over gin-smelling pine, sour poplar, and willow, stinking hemlock, and the horse-liniment smell of spruce. And somewhere along the way Paddy had once caught this peculiar smoke-sweat smell before. He glanced back and the collie was trying to sneak along behind. He gestured the dog back. If he didn't watch it Dorrga would be spoiled and useless.

His mount stepped daintily through packed snow, making no unnecessary noise. A hint of smoke rose straight from the stovepipe. So old Lawson was still here. . . . Paddy urged his horse toward the corral, praying the horses penned there would not be noisy greeting a stranger.

They weren't. The countryside was nearly light as day, but the corral had been churned into an unsavory mixture of mud and manure. He squinted into the patch of blackness. He could hear the quiet breathing of horses somewhere but could not see them. He half circled before they were visible in the moonlight—a pair of midnight blacks. He remembered from this morning the gray of old age about their muzzles. *Only two.* This morning there had been nineteen animals in this corral!

So that was why he was in such an unholy hurry to see me gone. He rode silently around the corral. The trail into the mountains was freshly churned. He dismounted and studied frozen hoofprints. Heavy-laden and unshod. And that smell lay heavier here between corral and sod house, where somebody had loaded the pack string. He picked up a trampled piece of pasteboard. A faint skim of clouds was crossing the moon now and he couldn't make out the printing. He sighed and stuffed it in his pocket. He was about to remount when he saw something else nearly invisible on the dirty snow. It was a feather.

So now what? He ought to be following that track up into the mountains to find out what kind of deviltry old Lawson was up to. But his kit was packed and ready back at the ranch. If he wasn't there come morning . . . He dropped the feather and got back onto his horse, trying to move as noiselessly as possible, but as he swung his leg up the leather of his new saddle picked that moment to creak like a rusty outhouse hinge.

Even before there was movement in the soddy the boy could *feel* it. He swung low on the far side, presenting only a hand on the saddle horn and the sole of one boot as he encouraged the horse away from the sod fort. He had covered fifty yards before the first shot whistled overhead. By the time the next round came he was far enough away to swing up into posting position and learn just how fast this horse could go. Without waiting for instructions, Dorrga joined him in full retreat.

Bad cess to this country's ways of welcoming strangers! Would he ever become inured to being shot at? Might get used to it someday, he decided. But Paddy didn't think he would ever learn to like it any more than he did coffee.

But thank the saints he was on a horse this time and it was only one rifle and that one not very well aimed. He didn't think Lawson had managed to get a glimpse of him—unless the old man had been awake and spying long before the saddle had decided to creak like that. But wouldn't Lawson guess? Maybe Paddy should have torn off in the opposite direction, the way those heavy-laden horses had gone. But even if there'd been time for mature decisions Paddy didn't know the country. Be a fine mess if he were to go that way and discover the only path back out was down this valley and past the fort again.

His hat had blown off and hung on his back. His ears

were freezing. He struggled to get his hat back on but the horse was young and full of vinegar and even after a couple of miles at full gallop showed no inclination to slow down. The collie had fallen back long ago. Served him right for not staying home in the warm when he'd had a chance. Finally the horse showed signs of having had enough. They were halfway back.

He decided he was safe. There had been only two not very good mounts in the corral and neither was saddled. He cooled out his horse and himself and, unless he was reading the moon wrong, it was not even midnight yet when he unsaddled and pushed his beast back into the Bar L corral. He put his tack on the rack and headed for the darkened bunkhouse. Cookie was not up yet. He was stepping quietly across the clearing when the bunkhouse door opened.

There was no place to hide. He was midway from corral to bunkhouse, in bright moonlight lit by snow. Whoever was opening the door had already seen him. The boy wracked his mind for an explanation. *I heard a noise and came out to see what was bothering the horses? I wanted to check my kit and see if I remembered matches? I thought I saw a falling star? I heard a banshee wail?*

The puncher coming out of the bunkhouse wore boots, long-handled underwear, and a denim jacket. "Cold like this and it gits damn hard to hold it all night," he said, and passed on, intent on his own affairs.

Paddy was having a similar problem. He slipped into the bunkhouse and undressed, trying not to awaken any of the other sleepers. It was not until he was under the blankets that he realized his dog had still not caught up. He tried to forget it. A border collie was used to living outside. No use spoiling the beast. The other man came in and went back to bed. The bunkhouse reverberated with snores.

Paddy lay staring ceilingward, wondering if he had been recognized out there at the fort. If the old man were to take out after him, would he cross paths with the dog? There were no other dogs about the Bar L. With a sinking feeling the boy knew that even if the old man had not seen him—even if Dorrga were to get here before the old firebrand were to saddle up and pursue him—how much intelligence would it take to connect up his daylight prying with this nocturnal follow-up?

Somebody's snoring reached a crescendo, degenerated into tooth grinding and muffled remarks about a goddamn tree-splitting cayuse. There were creaks and groans until it seemed as if everyone in the darkened room were turning over at once. He turned over too and tried to sleep. He didn't make it.

He lay tense, waiting for the sound of hoofbeats. That crazy old man had been ready to shoot him in broad daylight. In darkness he had not hesitated one instant to see if a creaking saddle might not signify innocent passage. That shot had come without warning, without any attempt to learn who or what was going on. Lawson might be old but he was still spry enough to ride. How long before he was here turning this bunkhouse inside out?

He had told Paddy to take what he needed and be on his way to Poplar Fork. Should he get out of bed and make tracks? His kit was ready. He could be on the trail in the time it took to saddle up and tie a diamond hitch. He tried to put himself into the old man's head. And decided that if he were not here the old rascal would trail him off into the wilderness and do him in without benefit of witnesses.

Lawson would assume he had departed the Bar L this afternoon—would suppose a boyish curiosity had gotten the best of him, that he had hidden his packhorses and kit somewhere long enough for a midnight detour up to the fort. Perhaps it would be best to stay here and pretend injured innocence. Then he remembered the puncher who had seen him outside. That man had assumed the boy was out on the same errand. But would he have been sleepy enough not to notice that Paddy was fully clothed?

His mind raced in circles like a pup worrying a goose. What kind of story must he make up and stick to? What did these riders know about him? He had told the black man about the incident in the sheep camp. But Brutus had been dead before Jug and Ottie showed up. They thought he had stumbled onto the dead sheep after the fact. Jug and Ottie were easy to fool—because they didn't really care. But was old Bill Lawson fooled? Somehow those glacial blue eyes did not seem trusting.

Jesus, Mary, and Joseph, he'd been in bed nigh onto half an hour and still he was puffing as if he'd sprinted all the way back from the fort! What had he forgotten? He had cooled out his horse and put it in the corral. His saddle was where the tack belonged. Was there any proof he had been away tonight? In all the haste he must have forgotten something. Thanks to the cord, he hadn't lost his hat. A glove? Had he left anything behind that would give him away when he tried to outdistance a bullet?

Any minute now, he told himself. He struggled for a properly sleepy look. Where was Dorrga? Waiting somewhere near the bunkhouse? Or would the old man find him on the road back down from the fort? He struggled to remind himself that he was twenty-one now. It was no longer fitting for him to flutter about like some sixteen-year-old squib of a groom.

Sounds carried amazingly in the cold night air. He could see moonlight through the single tiny bunkhouse window. And he could hear the galloping horse drawing rapidly closer. He turned face down and tried to breathe deeply, evenly. He struggled for a dazed, half-awake attitude. But even when he was expecting it the suddenness startled him as the bunkhouse door burst open and Lawson strode in with a rifle in his left hand and a coal-oil lantern in his right. As he stood silhouetted in the open doorway the collie slipped past him and scooted under Paddy's bunk.

Chapter 15

Sixteen years I'm waitin' for a bit o' luck and this is what I get! He lay face down, peeping under a raised arm as he tried to play possum. But how was it that all these thieves and murderers had clearer consciences than Paddy, who had never hurt anyone? The dozen other inhabitants of the bunkhouse were reacting with the patience and good humor that characterizes unexpected middle-of-the-night awakenings. "What the motherless hell's going on?" was one of their more subdued inquiries. Paddy decided he'd better wake up too. "Is it the Indians?" he demanded.

Lawson stood silent in the open doorway.

"Your firewood," a puncher finally growled. "Reckon you can try to warm the whole territory if you want to."

Lawson came in a step farther and closed the door. "What makes you think it's Indians?" He was looking straight at Paddy.

The boy opened his eyes all the way and glared right back. As rage boiled through him the fear was abruptly gone. "And would it be God-fearin' Christians makin' all this blather?" he railed. "That's twice today ye've pointed that fool thing at me. And me a landowner! Don't ye know guns are dangerous? In Ireland they're used to kill people and 'tis not thought neighborly to—"

As he lit into the old man, his voice rising with each word, Paddy suddenly noted that he was sounding very like his mother whenever Paddy tracked mud into her kitchen. And the mad old man with rifle and lantern was reacting just as Paddy did whenever his mother inventoried the obstacles that were accumulating between the boy and the Kingdom of Heaven.

The dozen other men in the bunkhouse were also inflated with righteous anger until an impartial observer might never have guessed that their chorus of inspired invective was aimed at the man who paid their wages, whom they had loyally followed into town and backed up against a hostile mob of nesters.

White hair bristling like a hedgehog, the old man weathered their cursing like a mule in a hailstorm. "Enough!" he finally roared. There was still sufficient of the old bucko in him for the abuse to stop immediately. "Who's been out of here tonight?" he growled in the sudden silence.

The cowboys were mystified. "Now what in hell kind of question is that?" one asked.

"It's a simple one and I want an answer."

"Just about everybody, I'd reckon," another puncher added. "When you gonna put an indoor privy in this boar's nest?"

"What're *you* doin' here?" This time Lawson was talking straight at Paddy.

"I was sleepin' till a minute ago," the boy said pointedly. "'Tis a long ride I've got tomorrow. But if it's a crazy old man can't remember where he sent me, then you'd best give me a shilling and I'll be off in another direction."

"You can give me my time too," a grizzled puncher growled. "Think I'll go with him."

"When you gonna put some steam heat in here?" somebody asked.

"And a bathtub?"

Lawson emitted a disgusted growl and left the bunkhouse, taking rifle and lantern with him. Somebody lit the lamp.

"You shore talked up to him, boy." It was the one who had surprised Paddy coming in.

Dazedly, Paddy realized that he had. What had come over him? He would never have dared raise his voice to his gentleman, and his gentleman had never once pointed a pistol at him. Had he singly turned all these men against the boss of the Bar L? It was a heady experience. Was this the way a man got his start in politics?

But while he tried to digest what had happened the boy gradually realized it was all just talk. Nobody was going to quit. Tomorrow life at the Bar L would go on as usual. Had he fooled old Lawson? Talk died down and the lamp was blown out again. Still the boy lay sleepless. The dog . . . had Lawson come across him out on the trail to the fort? Or had the collie just been waiting outside for somebody to open the door?

It was hard for the boy to understand these men. He knew horses. At his gentleman's estate there had been a stallion who learned to gallop under a low-lying limb and scrape off his rider. He killed two men. Paddy remembered the look of supercilious cunning. Those stallion eyes had known they were putting something over—right up until the instant of blank surprise when a bullet made a third eye between them. It was the same look of half-mad scheming he had seen in old Lawson. Did the Bar L's forty men know they were working for a lunatic? Or were they still bedazzled by the great things Lawson had done when he was younger, saner, before the lesser breeds began snapping at his heels?

Morning. Final breakfast in the cookhouse, and hit the trail. There was a hint of warmth in the air. Not thawing, but the horses were not quite so stiff-legged. It had not snowed since before Jug and Ottie had "rescued" him up at Poplar Fork, so the straight miles of trail along the sunken creek and fence posts were already broken from their ride in, plus Jug and Ottie's return ride to the line cabin, where they were stretching barbed wire.

He made camp early on the afternoon of the second day because the last of his cookhouse bread was gone. He had watched Ottie's skill with a dutch oven and now he struggled to produce something he had not tasted since his mother's in County Down. The soda bread was just near enough to the real thing for the boy to be so suddenly overwhelmed that he buried his face in the mane of his roan and wept. The collie, being Scotch, diplomatically pretended an interest in a snowshoe rabbit's tracks.

When he arrived the next day the cabin was there but Jug and Ottie were not. Off building fence, he supposed. There was a haystack by their corral and only one horse penned there. He rearranged his lightened loads onto the larger of his packhorses and left the other in the corral. He reminded himself that these men were thieves and murderers, had killed the old Scotsman and tried to kill him. Still, the boy was tempted to stay the night. But in the end he knew that it would only be that much harder if he dawdled now.

He made nearly ten more miles up the creek before the heavy-laden horse showed signs of—not rebellion. Mules might refuse to carry more than they deemed proper. But horses share with men a propensity for working themselves to death. He was moving down to camp in the poplars by the creek when a deer erupted, bouncing along in twenty-foot broad jumps. The boy was so startled that the animal was out of sight before he even remembered the Peacemaker strapped to his waist. He began making camp.

The first day out Paddy had talked to the dog and to his horses, but none of them were much for small talk. Gradually he slipped back into the dour silence that is so much a part of being Irish. Remembering how Himself would return to the cottage and spend an evening in total harmony with his family and not saying a dozen words all night, Paddy wondered how it had ever gotten about that they were a talkative people.

Next day he reached the fork where he had made a lean-to for the black man's final hours. Had he, perhaps, been too hard? He remembered the Scotsman who had taught him to shoot a sawed-off Tower musket. So here he was alone again and nothing but a Colt. Why couldn't he have demanded a rifle as long as he was lighting into old Lawson?

The way he'd had the old bucko on the run he might have been able to possess himself of the same rifle that had shot at him.

Snow filtered down through the branches that roofed the lean-to. He considered pitching his tent in the middle of the rectangle where someone had laid out a cabin, then realized that with no one to help him, he could easily let slip a log and end up with neither cabin nor tent. He chopped fresh brush to spread on the snow, put his ground cloth over it, and pitched his tent elsewhere.

Hobbled horses were pricking their ears and showing too much white of eye. Paddy worried. He had not yet encountered a bear nor any of those local animals that Mr. Bridgeman had assured him with a perfectly straight face were as big as a lion or a tiger. He hated to keep the horses hobbled, but if he didn't he would be in for a long walk come springtime. Maybe the smoke of the campfire would keep whatever it was away. Couldn't be a bear, he decided —unless Mr. Bridgeman had been drawing the long bow again about their way of sleeping all winter.

By next morning, whatever it was must have moved on, for the horses now grazed unconcernedly wherever they could paw the snow away. He had a sack of oats but that had to be saved for emergencies. January . . . if the men in the bunkhouse were telling the truth he was in for four more months of snow, then a month of mud before it would be possible to ride out of here. He consoled himself with the knowledge that Jug and Ottie's cabin was much closer. And after all, he had been ready to walk out of here barefoot once already. He started dragging and prying logs together for a cabin.

It would have been impossible to work alone if this were properly timbered country, but the logs that somebody had piled up years ago were a mixed bag of poplar and lodgepole; they were well dried, and the thickest was barely six inches. They were trimmed and notched already, so he decided to build the cabin to preplanned size even if it would be twice as big as he could ever need.

There was a separate pile of yard-long notched logs and others somewhat longer. He puzzled over their proper use and tried laying his material out this way and that. Nothing worked. It was not until he had laid a couple of courses that the boy realized what was wrong. He took it all apart and began laying his walls with a fireplace in one end, and now the yard-long notched logs made sense. The only thing he could not see was how he was going to keep a wooden chimney from burning up.

He was starting again when he realized that even dry, a six-inch lodgepole is near the limit for one man to lift. But the poplars after years of drying were almost weightless. He could use the pine first and save the poplar for roof and upper walls. In spite of false starts and fumbles the walls were knee high before it was time to see to the horses and boil the kettle.

It was a week before the rafters were up. He knew how to tie thatch, but what grass this country offered was short and beneath knee-deep snow. He studied half-yard-long baulks somebody had sawed from the largest tree in this region— nearly a foot thick at the butt—and guessed he would have to learn to use the tool the Bar L farrier had insisted he take along with saw and ax.

The froe was a treacherous-looking piece of iron, sharp on one side, and it vaguely resembled a sickle whose blade had been uncurled into a straight line. But when he experimented by laying it on the end of a baulk and banging the froe with a club, the shakes split off clean. He laid a row, counted, and tried to guess how many to finish the roof. A second count and he knew he dared not use more than one nail apiece.

The weather held clear and cold, which was why the shakes split so beautifully clean and smoother than ever wood will split in warm weather. Mornings the flap of his tent would be rimed with frost from his breath, but it did not snow. He had lost count again but it had to be nearing February. And the worst of winter still to come.

The roof was on, door hinged, and window framed and awaiting a pane of unhaired rabbit skin before it finally snowed again, scarcely enough to cover old tracks. He caught his horse and splashed up and down the ice-rimmed creek inspecting mudbanks and finally found one of a promising clay.

The chimney was wide enough to stand inside, but despite these ample dimensions the boy had more clay on himself than he did on the logs by the time he had finished. And he suspected most of it was frozen in place rather than properly plastered. He built a tiny fire and waited to see what happened.

What happened was a mudslide. He spent a week plastering and patching after each fire and still could not trust it. "Forst time I build enough fire to warm me toes this whole cabin's up in smoke," he growled. The collie studied him mournfully and thumped his tail.

Paddy studied dwindling stores and counted the ribs of his horses. He pitched his tent inside the cabin that night and built a campfire in the middle of the floor instead of in the fireplace. Smoke oozed through the shake roof easily enough. What more could he do here? He studied the wood-and-mud chimney. There must be a way to build these things and make them work, but he didn't know how. He was just dropping off to sleep when he abruptly realized he had been reading something into his orders that was not strictly there.

Lawson sent him up here to build a cabin, not to remain all winter. Once somebody packed in a tin stove and some pipe this cabin would be as good as any. And the snow was still only a couple of inches deeper than when he had ridden in.

"Ready to leave?" he asked.

Chapter 16

Dorrga didn't seem taken with the idea. He pricked his ears and growled. Next morning it had snowed another light, powdery inch. He strapped on his Peacemaker and stepped outside to see what else the collie had to growl about.

Suddenly he remembered this was the place where he had buried the black man under a pile of rocks. The temperature had not risen above thawing in the time the boy had been back, but . . . Paddy didn't believe in ghosts. He was almost sure they didn't exist. So what bothered the dog last night? Paddy squinted into dazzling sunlight. There would never be a better time to look over Brutus' grave.

This morning for once his horses were in plain sight. He studied their prominent ribs and knew it was time to dole out oats if he were to make it back to Jug and Ottie and the small haystack by their corral. Then as he neared the gravesite Paddy saw the extra horse.

For an instant he thought his "rescuers" were paying another visit; then he knew this shaggy, chronically starved animal could not be a Bar L horse. Its ears were notched but it was unshod and without a brand. He would have taken it for one of the wild horses Mr. Bridgeman was always talking about were it not for the white patches on its back, which were the indelible traces of a pack saddle. The beast was not hobbled but it was so bedraggled it had to be a stray. He wished he could spare a peck of oats. But oats would kill any horse in this famished condition.

Then he noted that this shaggy creature midway between horse and pony seemed to be fending perfectly well for itself, pawing energetically to sheep off grass in places where his larger Bar L horses had long since given up. Paddy came as close as the strange horse would let him and searched for signs of ownership. Apart from notched ears there were none.

It wasn't till he turned back to the cabin that the boy discovered the horse had not come alone. Two bundles of rags huddled together under the eave on the far side from the door.

Jesus, Mary, and Joseph! After all the worrying he'd done about Indians . . . Not that these wretched creatures seemed any threat. Dorrga growled. A head emerged from the smaller bundle and Paddy recoiled from the aura of unwashed humanity. Did all Indians smell like this?

Then he remembered it had been a month since his own last bath and change. Was this boy asking himself the same questions about the Irish? The boy saw the Peacemaker at Paddy's belt and hands emerged from his blanket to point skyward. He said something that sounded like *"Tillicum."*

"And I don't suppose there's a hope in hell of yez speakin' any Christian tongue?"

"No shoot," the boy pleaded. "Me good."

The other bundle of rags began moving. The head that emerged was black, with twin braids like the boy's, but this was an older man. He looked up and his face was so deformed Paddy could not imagine how he could be still alive. It took a moment to understand the look of sudden recognition in those pain-ridden eyes. It was Lumpjaw!

This was the Indian—one of them, anyway—who had stolen his horses, killed his gentleman and Mr. Bridgeman. The last time Paddy had seen him it had looked as if he might have a slight toothache. Now he couldn't even close his mouth. Paddy caught another rank whiff and knew it wasn't the boy. It was Lumpjaw who emitted the odor of death. "Yes," Paddy said. "I know you too."

If Lumpjaw did not understand, at least he sensed the quiet satisfaction. Paddy was suddenly shaken with a rage that had almost left him during the busy time of cabin-building. Now every moment of terror and misery was once more vivid in his mind: burying his gentleman and Mr. Bridgeman, struggling to get down the mountain, the sheep-camp massacre. If it weren't for this misshapen lump of wretchedness Paddy would be back in County Down by now. He caressed the butt of the Peacemaker.

Lumpjaw began to chant. Paddy was suddenly stricken with the symmetry of God's work. The last time it was this man who had watched with detached curiosity as Paddy said an Act of Contrition.

The symmetry ended there. Paddy had been fifteen, in health, and with the hope that God might give him a long life. Since he had last seen Lumpjaw the Indian's glossy hair had thinned and was now dusty with gray. His eyes were dulled from constant pain, and only a mouth that could not chew would explain his emaciation. Nothing Paddy could devise would equal the punishment this man's creator had found fitting to visit upon him. He took his hand from the pistol.

Lumpjaw's death song went on interminably while Dorrga hunched beside Paddy, emitting an antiphony of growls. The younger Indian maintained a respectful silence. Upstream a horse blew and spun as if ten thousand devils were on his tail. And still Lumpjaw chanted as if this noise were necessary to round out the balance of his private universe.

What on earth was Paddy going to do with two indigent Indians? He barely had food for himself and Dorrga. Besides, he had planned on leaving this morning. The chanting finally ended and Lumpjaw, peace on his ruined face, sat with a certain equanimity. Paddy emerged from his own thoughts to see what the older Indian was waiting for. He shook his head. "Do your own dirty work," he growled.

Sun began reaching down into the poplars, but the three of them were shadowed on the north side of the cabin. Paddy stepped out to warm himself, and the boy followed. Lumpjaw did not. Paddy stood dithering. What was he going to do with these strays? He had been lonely, often thought how nice it would be to have a companion of his own age, but—. He sighed. There was only one thing he could do this time of day: Fix breakfast.

The sun was positively warm this morning in spite of last night's snowfall. He was damned if he would piddle about with that untrustworthy fireplace. Besides, he didn't want the smell of a moribund Lumpjaw inside his cabin. The boy followed him to the door and stood waiting with the same air of melancholy hope that he occasionally surprised on the collie's face when it had been a long time between meals. Paddy kicked snow from the ring of stones in front of the cabin door and made wood-gathering gestures. Immediately the Indian boy was moving. The arms and legs that flashed from his blanket were thin as a potato planter's during the Hunger.

Though Paddy liked his oats with substance, he boiled them thin and soupy in deference to Lumpjaw. He added a lump of coarse, not-quite-white sugar and set out four bowls. The Indian boy took two and went around back of the cabin. Paddy and his dog finished theirs in the sunlight. He sat staring at the dog, wondering what next. He could not bring himself to kill this wreck of the man who had stolen his youth.

And what were those blatherskites up to behind the cabin? Couldn't take even a lumpy-jawed Indian this long to scoff down a bowl of gruel. He checked the Peacemaker—as if he hadn't rechecked it a dozen times already—and eased his quiet way around the cabin. Bedad, and was it ever cold in the shade!

The boy sat facing Lumpjaw, who had not moved since finishing his death song. The boy's bowl was empty. The older Indian's was untouched.

Paddy remembered the black man. Brutus had been a man of mature years and wisdom. He had known when to quit. Paddy hoped that, no matter what the priests might blather, he would have sense enough when the time came to do the same. He took the bowls back to the front of the cabin where Dorrga, untroubled by etiquette or omens, did not hesitate to scoff down the food the Indian had refused.

The boy reappeared. Paddy handed him the dishes and directed him to the creek. Paddy busied himself with chores and tried not to make any plans. If he did nothing long enough, perhaps things would take care of themselves. His horses were getting into scandalous shape. He studied their ribs and balanced distance against his limited supply of oats. There was but one way he could get the maximum benefit of the feed into his horses. He boiled up another batch of sugared gruel for them and thus circumvented the oats' survival technique of passing undigested through a horse to sprout once again in another pasture. The Bar L animals finished off their half buckets before they had properly cooled. The Indian pony was not even curious.

The boy pursued Paddy with the persistence of a bailiff, struggling to make himself useful and working with a willingness not to be found in the unstarved. "Where'd you come from?" Paddy asked.

"Me good. Me work."

Paddy repeated the question in Irish and got the same reply. He tried again slowly in English. He drew figures in the snow of two men on a horse, pointed at the boy and at the line he traced behind the horse.

The boy studied the drawing a moment, then pointed at the sun and held up eight fingers.

"Not how long," Paddy growled. "Where?" He took the stick again and drew a circle at the far end of the line behind the horse. Something in the boy's manner told him the young Indian understood him well enough. But the boy did not want to say where he had come from. Paddy shrugged and got to his feet. "Ye've just punched out the last hole in your meal ticket," he growled. To hell with them. These savages were not his responsibility. They'd gotten here on their own. They could get somewhere else and be thankful he didn't kill them!

But the boy was beside him again, tugging timidly at his sleeve. He took a stick and drew in the snow. It was a time before Paddy understood what the joining lines meant. Then the boy drew in the rectangle of the cabin, pointed at Paddy, at himself. Finally Paddy decided the boy was trying to explain that they were not coming *from* anywhere, that the boy and the ailing older Indian were on their way *to* a place—to Poplar Fork. He remembered the arrowhead he had picked up here.

"Ain't no Injuns around this country," Mr. Bridgeman had said—before he ended up scalped. Perhaps not. Or there were so few and so demoralized they were not considered a threat. But there had been Indians here. He had wondered when he picked up the arrowhead if he was walking on some Indian's grave. Which explained Lumpjaw's equanimity when he faced Paddy's pistol. The Indian had come here to die.

"Foot Lodge," the boy said. Paddy stared and the boy repeated it. He pointed at the circle Paddy had scratched at the beginning of their journey. So what and where was foot lodge? There was not enough language between them for Paddy ever to find out.

"What's wrong with Lumpjaw?" he asked.

The boy didn't understand the question, but he must have heard somebody call the older man by that name. He touched his jaw and made a wincing movement. Paddy nodded.

"All die," the boy said.

Now what did that mean? Lumpjaw is a disease that afflicts cattle. Paddy knew that on rare occasions the fungal infection could get into humans but it was not the sort of thing that would spread like the pox or other plagues. He remembered the first time he had seen the older man. Looked like a toothache then. It didn't take a doctor or even a groom to know now that the Indian was dying of cancer. "All die?" Paddy repeated.

The boy assured him that he had understood correctly.

Paddy managed in the course of his chores to get a look at the older man every half hour or so. Lumpjaw sat motionless on the cold side of the cabin, eyes open but no longer seeing. His blankets were slowly falling open and the way he sat motionless in the shade, it could not be long before he would accomplish his purpose. Paddy wondered if someday he would be privileged to go back to County Down and die in familiar surroundings. But mostly, he wondered how long he was going to have to hang around here in Poplar Fork eating up scarce provisions and starving his horses. Sooner or later winter would settle down with a vengeance and if he didn't take advantage of the fine weather now he would have no excuse for complaining.

What more could he do? He had built the cabin. There was nothing he could do to improve the dam as long as the ground was frozen harder than a landlord's heart.

But no matter how he might fume and mutter, he could not just ride off and leave the old man to die. He put his kit together, except the saw and ax, which might as well stay in the cabin. His saddlebags were ready when noon came but still old Lumpjaw clung to life, staring unseeing into the northern sky. Noon passed and it would be too late to start by the time . . . Muttering to himself, Paddy unpacked sufficient gear to boil jerked beef and rice.

The dog seemed to share his impatience to be gone of this place before the weather changed. He no longer growled at the Indians but all day long the dog had pointed his nose upstream, sniffing the north wind and growling. Toward afternoon the dog's excitement grew.

Paddy wondered if the collie could smell a storm coming. The Indian boy was watching too. He seemed as nervous as the dog. "What is it?" Paddy demanded. "Will it snow?"

"Foot lodge," the boy said.

"Go wash your feet if they're cold." Paddy went out to bring in more firewood. He caught another glimpse of Lumpjaw still squatting erect as a Buddha. The Indian had thrown off his blanket and sat naked in the freezing air.

Paddy thrust his armload of wood inside the cabin and went out for more. He beckoned the boy to follow and help.

"Foot lodge," the boy repeated. "All die."

"So you all died of lumpjaw," Paddy growled. "'Tis of cold we'll all be dyin' here if you don't get some fuel put aside." They crossed the creek at a narrow point and ranged out of the land enclosed by the fork to hunt more wood. Dorrga followed, whining in a most unstoical fashion. "And what's botherin' you?" Paddy snarled. "Don't yez think I've enough on me mind?"

He was about to enlarge on this theme when the shooting started. It sounded like at least a dozen men popping away back in Poplar Fork. The Indian boy disappeared. Irrelevantly, at that moment Paddy finally understood what he had been saying about "foot lodge." The boy had been doing his best to pronounce "Fort Rudge."

Chapter 17

Paddy grabbed the dog and pulled him into the underbrush. Rifles popped away like soldiers target shooting as boy and dog wormed backward to bury themselves. He felt the Peacemaker. *Fort Rudge; all die.* Had the Indians come out in force to wipe out an Army post? Paddy supposed it was possible. Men would get used to routine, permit Indians inside the gates to traffic in women or other merchandise, and sooner or later one fine day . . .

But why was Lumpjaw here? To die, of course. Might be no connection. The boy's hangdog air? Paddy had not been all that cheerful when he learned his father had finally lost a game of wits with a horse. Chances were the rest of the savages were not starving. They'd be feeling their oats back near the scene of their triumph. Except the ones who'd come this way.

As suddenly as it began, the shooting stopped. Dorrga whined. Paddy whapped him over the muzzle and the dog apologized. They lay silent in their brushy tunnel and waited. He counted the extra cartridges in his pocket, glad now that he had not wasted one on Lumpjaw, who was ready to die anyhow. He could never get them all but he intended to get one of those murdering savages before they got him. That bellwether of a boy had begged his food and hospitality. *Kick meself for not killin' the pair of thim!*

Half an eternity passed, though he supposed it could not have been more than five minutes. He could hear the creak of saddlery and the sounds of horses as men ranged about his cabin. Then, just as he was reminding himself that Indians do not use saddles, the boy's growing suspicions were corroborated by the sound of a bugle.

And now he knew what they had been shooting at. Soldiers riding down the creek, coming from Fort Rudge. Soldiers see an Indian. He wondered if Lumpjaw had been already dead before these trigger-happy cavalrymen riddled him. He took a deep breath and yelled.

"Is it Christian men ye are? If you're all through makin' holes in me cabin I'd like to come in out o' the cold."

"Who is it?"

"'Tis the inscribed and legal owner o' Poplar Fork," he shouted back, "and I'll thank yez not to be shootin' at me."

There was some muttering about goddamn Irish and a sharp reply. And then finally an answering shout, only this one was, *"Kaen foodhar athaw footh a-nish?"*

"A fine one y'are t' be askin' me what *I'm* up to! And you an Irishman. 'Tis a great shame on yez t' be shootin' in daycent people's houses!"

Moments later he was back in front of his cabin and facing up to a lieutenant who did not seem that much older than Paddy—a fault which the lieutenant attempted to remedy with a marginally successful mustache. But the lieutenant's eyes were hard and cold. "Where's the other one?" he demanded.

So it wasn't the soldiers who had all died. No wonder the Indian boy had been looking nervously up the creek all morning. "If you're talkin' about that miserable savage came back here to die," Paddy said, "I'd not waste good powder on somethin' God was doin' nicely with no help from me."

"The other one?" the lieutenant repeated.

"All thim rifles poppin' away without once lookin'. I find ye've killed a Bar L harse and thin ye'll be for it!"

"Where's the other one?"

"Old Man Lawson'll be havin' yer guts for garters," Paddy promised.

So they were bivouacked in Paddy's clearing and Paddy's Peacemaker was in the lieutenant's possession and Paddy and his dog were prisoners in his own cabin and bad cess to the lot of them. But whatever had brought a troop of cavalry clear up over the mountains this time of year? Surely not just two Indians. There were tents and fires outside and soon he smelled cooking. Damn them all! What had that Indian boy done to draw this wrath upon him? Ruefully, Paddy reflected that life here must be as difficult for an Indian as it was for an Irishman since the English had invaded. *Damn them all!*

The door opened and an aging man in civilian clothes brought a mug of coffee and a plate of stew. As he put them down Paddy knew there was something familiar about the old man. Willing to swear he had seen him before. Dorrga shot forward like a cannon ball, nearly knocking the old man down. It was the sheepherder who had taught the boy to shoot a Tower musket.

"Ye're a quick learner," the old man said dryly.

"And here I was not knowin' if ye were in Scotland or in Heaven!" Paddy thought a moment and added, "There's a man and horse here both dead thanks to you."

"Is there now? And do the rest of the Bar L know you're here?"

"'Tis one o' their landowners I am now," Paddy said and told the Scotsman everything that had happened since the night Bar L shot up the sheep camp.

"And they don't know you were wi' me?"

Paddy assured him they did not. "And what are ye doin' here with all these galloglass goons?"

"Guidin' them back through the mountains."

"And why would a soldier leave a snug fort this time o' year?"

"Why would anybody give the Indians a better kind o' rifle than soldiers carry?" the old man asked. "If the puir savages were not convinced that raisin' the sights makes a gun shoot harder, there might ha' been more bluid shed."

"And wasn't there?" Paddy was remembering the boy's "All die."

"Oh aye," the old man sighed. "Soldiers sit around wi' naught to do and they recall somebody was killed while killin' Indians and one thing leads to another. 'Tis not those puir savages camped round the fort and half starved from bad beef that're to blame. If there's burnin' in Hell to do, 'tis for the man furnished the guns—the man told the story and sold the shirts to stop bullets. Now tell me, lad, who'd do a thing like that?"

Paddy was floundering in new depths of evil. "Who?" he echoed. But it was a rhetorical question. Surely things like this didn't happen. Not even the English— "But why're ye not home in Roscommon?"

"And leave me sheep?"

"Yours?"

"Aye. I didna' tell ye that, did I?"

"Does any man tell the truth in this country?"

"No more than necessary," the old man said. "Nor more than in any other country, includin' yours, if ye'll think about it."

Paddy wondered how many more things he had not been told. Now that he considered, it was a reasonable precaution for the old man to disown a herd of sheep if immediate hanging or shooting were the consequence of admitting he was not just a poor man doing his job. "But I don't like bein' lied to," Paddy grumped.

"Neither does that soldier lad. And that's why I'm sent in here—to sweet-talk you and find out why you're hidin' the boy. His tracks are a' about the place."

Paddy had not thought of that. He sighed. How to explain a whim? "Damned stiff-necked galloglass!" he snarled. "Huntin' down a gossoon can't be as old as I was when—"

Suddenly the old Scotsman's reserve melted. "But wasna' the old one the same as did ye dastardly in the mountains?"

"Dyin' he was. Maybe dead before all those bullets hit him."

"Aye. And now they know it. They're also seein' now they had no call to kill women and children. They're shamed men a-lookin' for a scapegoat and ye'd best no' go rubbin' any noses in what they've done."

Paddy started to answer and he was lost in thought. Was anything as it seemed in this country? Did anyone tell the whole truth? Had he? Had he told Lawson or the Bar L men about his connection with the sheep camp? It had been a dying black man—whom he had treated with no kindness— who warned him not to tell. Then he realized the Scotsman had still not explained why he was still in the territory after all this time.

"Aye," the old man agreed, "a long time. But remember, soldier lads couldna' care less if it's sheep or cattle have the country. 'Twas no' till somebody armed the Indians that soldiers commenced to see their duty."

So that was the way it was. "And will they be thinkin' I was the one? Don't they know what Indians did to me and my gentleman?" But there was still something askew. "All these soldiers chasin' after a dyin' man and a boy?" But even as he said it, Paddy was remembering which of the people in this country had laughed at the thought of Indians—and which had shown no surprise at the thought of a lumpy-jawed Indian. "You and I know," he guessed. "Do they?"

The old man gave a dry cackle. "If they don't, 'tis no' for lack of me tellin' them. But knowin's one thing and provin's another."

Paddy wondered if the soldiery had been equally nice over whether to shoot all the Indians.

The old man seemed to read his mind. "Puir bluidy savages starvin' under the guns o' the fort. 'Twas enough to make a man think o' the Highlands after the forty-five." He sighed. "Soldiers rememberin' Custer and Cawnpore and God kens what goes through a soldier's head. Then a big stomp dance a' night and a yowlin' that'd kill a cat and come mornin' the lads in the fort looked out and saw them a' wi' new rifles and it must ha' seemed the answer to a soldier's prayer."

"All dead?"

"They're brave men but no' hopeless daft. 'Twas mostly the women and children, some of the old men that I saw dead."

"And now they're out chasin' them. But 'twas only the two came this way."

"No, lad. 'Tis the guns they're after."

"But they had none. Would I be alive if they'd had?"

"What d'ye suppose old Lumpjaw and a' them heavy-laden horses were up to in the mountains the day the puir old savage saved your life and sent you away from seein' what the pack train was carryin'?"

While Paddy was digesting this the old man added, "Could ye swear now that a' the men runnin' that pack string were Indians?"

So that was what sent a troop of cavalry out in midwinter. He finished off the stew the old man had brought and gulped down the coffee, wondering absently if ever he would come to like this bitter brew. Was there anything about this country that was not bitter? Guilt, vengeance were woven as deeply into the fabric of being here as they were in Ireland. And this land had less than two generations of history!

And now I'll be losin' me dog, he thought as the Scotsman took plate and cup and went out of the cabin with Dorrga on his heels.

Moments later a soldier stuck his head in. "You can come out now," he growled.

Paddy didn't much feel like coming out but the dog had gone so he might as well. He wondered if the Indian boy had managed to connect up with his pony and get well away. But mostly Paddy wondered what he was going to do. He had been laying great bloody plans to avenge an humble shepherd who had turned out not so humble nor in all that much need of help. The Bar L men had killed a few sheep and given Paddy a scare. It was difficult to sustain a fine rage against anyone for what were essentially pranks. And what with all these dams and improvements, perhaps old Bill Lawson . . . half-mad old man . . . But didn't he have as much right to protect his property as anyone?

An hour ago Paddy had known exactly where he stood: alone against the world—against the townspeople of Ruby and, more specifically, against the all-encircling tentacles of the Bar L. Now . . .

But the Scotsman was right—providing this time it was the whole truth. To arm Indians was a disservice to any Christian. Nor was it any help to the poor savages, since to give them arms was merely to give a less forgiving race an excuse to finish them off. It seemed, to Paddy, a singularly Irish situation.

Where did he stand? Squarely in the middle, where he had been since the first day he set foot in this bloody country. The Scotsman had fed him, taught him to shoot—had even, Paddy abruptly realized, offered to make him an heir. It wasn't somebody else's sheep the old man had offered to give him. It was his own!

And what of the simple-minded Bar L assassins? The black man had done his best to set the boy straight—warned him what not to say. Jug, Ottie—every one of those murderers had excellent reasons for not wanting Paddy alive to testify. So he had ended up with a new saddle, new clothes, new mackinaw—even if it did have an unsewn and bottomless pocket—and here he was a landowner! It was enough to make a man think.

Still thinking, he stepped outside. Tents and fires filled the small open space in front of the cabin. It was getting dark already and promised to be even colder tonight. He circled the cabin and even in gathering darkness could see bullet nicks in the lodgepoles. There was no blood where Lumpjaw had sat all day waiting to die. Must have been frozen stiff before the first bullet touched him. Gone now.

Not even a ghost.

But as Paddy stood under the eaves of his cabin he sensed

that there was a ghost. He remembered the overpowering stench when the old Indian had been alive. It was still here. Not so all-pervading now. But now Paddy knew where he had smelled that sweet-smoke-sweat stink before.

Chapter 18

So what did it prove? You couldn't convict a man on a smell. Paddy had been mistaken so many times already he knew how easily he could be wrong about this. He went out in the last of the light to see to his horses, suddenly afraid they would not be there. Then he realized the Indian boy would have been more concerned with getting away. It would have been pointless for him to steal Paddy's horses knowing the cavalry troop had more.

There was no sign of the Indian pony but he saw unshod tracks heading downstream until they were lost in the tiny, still unfrozen part of the creek. Why would the boy head downstream? No reason, Paddy decided, except that with soldiers behind there was no other way to run. At the first opportunity the Indian boy would backtrack, and snow or none, the hopes of finding him would be those of a potato in Dublin. Paddy went back into the cabin and tried to sleep.

He supposed he had, for suddenly it was morning and soldiers blathering about and one came in to tell him to get a wiggle on and saddle up.

"Where we goin'?"

"I don't even know where we been," the soldier replied.

They rode downstream and two days later the troop pulled up at Jug and Ottie's cabin. There was no sign of either. The corral was empty. So was the haystack. Paddy remembered how old Lawson had assured him of help here if anything went wrong. Had the old bastard sent him up Poplar Fork to die? Why had his winter's grub supply gone so quickly?

By now the young lieutenant had gotten over his huff

and, constrained from easy converse with mere enlisted men, encouraged Paddy and the Scotsman to ride with him at the head of the column. When they headed downstream from the line cabin Paddy asked, "Why would a whole troop be followin' a single horse?"

The lieutenant gave him an odd look but didn't answer.

"'Twas no' a single horse when we started out," the old Scotsman explained.

"If a lot o' them started off, then why aren't yez chasin' the lot instead o' this one?"

The lieutenant's explanations were complex and embarrassing. From what Paddy made of it, tracks had diminished so gradually that they had been nearing the pass where he buried his gentleman, breathing raggedly and horses near wilting before someone noticed that the tracks were markedly fewer.

One by one, Indians had slipped away from the main body, sweeping out their tracks, and the young lieutenant, facing freezing disaster in the mountains, had been forced to follow the remaining tracks, which dwindled each day until now he was on the same wild-goose chase after a single horse but there was nothing to do but go on unless he wished to go back over the mountains this time of year.

Apart from an excellent chance of freezing to death, the lieutenant was unwilling to face the possibility of mass desertion. But since he did not admit these reasons even to himself, it took Paddy most of one day to work it out even with the aid of an occasional half smile from the old man on the lieutenant's opposite side.

"D'you know Lawson?" Paddy asked the Scotsman.

"We're old acquaintances."

Paddy waited till the lieutenant had to drop to the rear of the column for some reason and then in rapid Irish: "Thoud'st not be having a look in the ogre's den wer't not for these many guns. Will the galloglasses be knowin' how old Lawson will give thee greeting?"

"'Tis their line o' work," the old man said dryly.

Paddy began to wonder if he might not better have raised such a fuss that the lieutenant would have left him to freeze uneventfully at Poplar Fork. Then he remembered the disappearing tracks. Somewhere loose in this country was a band of warriors who had just seen white men kill their women, their children, their old. He remembered the empty corral at the line cabin. Where were Jug and Ottie?

Where was Paddy?

Soldiers had killed the poor savages. Been itching for the chance since some mad goldilocks of a general had sacrificed his men to his vanity. But who had given the soldiers their excuse? The boy rode wrapped in his own dark thoughts. If they'd have him—and if he weren't so tired of being always on the losing side—bedamned if he wouldn't join the Indians!

Later he thought to ask another question: "How many Indians were camped around Fort Rudge?"

The lieutenant considered a moment. "Maybe three thousand."

"And would ye be thinkin' one out of four was a fightin' man?"

It appeared that the lieutenant would be so thinking.

"And how many of yez in the fort?"

"Between expired enlistments and the grippe there couldn't have been over a couple of hundred effectives."

"And thim savages standin' still while ye charged out and trained cannon?"

"I see what you're getting at," the lieutenant said. "Nearly three times as many of them, and with better rifles. Would have been a different story if their ammunition had been as good."

Paddy glanced at the old Scotsman who added, "Not American; not British. Rifles were new bu' the cartridges—" He shrugged.

"French label," the lieutenant said. "But I'd guess it was Belgian or somesuch off brand. Half of it wouldn't go off and the rest barely made it out the barrel."

To Paddy it looked as if someone had coppered his bets. There had been no possible way for the Indians to win. He gave the Scotsman a sidelong look as he wondered if the soldiers would be properly appreciative of this favor. But by now Paddy had learned not to give voice to everything that crossed his mind. He was still struggling to sift truth from poetry when they passed another of his campsites on the way up. Everything was as he had left it, save that now the tracks were beyond following. There were times when he thought he could make out the unshod hoofprints of an Indian pony, but other horses, cows, even what looked like a mule had passed along this trail until there was no certainty.

Then the main ranch of the Bar L lay ahead of them. Paddy remembered how he had ridden into Ruby expecting to be shot at any moment. What would happen this time? The only thing that happened was a royal welcome as the dozen-odd punchers in the bunkhouse turned out to make the soldiers comfortable and feed their oatbound horses carefully measured stooks of hay.

The troopers set up behind the cookhouse and the Scotsman stuck close by. Paddy had been watching for any sign of recognition but none of the Bar L riders seemed to know the old man. Paddy recalled how he had nearly not known the old shepherd himself. Most marvelous what a change of clothes and trim of beard could do. *Haircut an' some clean clothes an' you a gentleman. Ain't nothin' ever gonna make me white.*

Once more Paddy dithered. Bar L men would surely think it odd if he bunked out here with the troopers. What would the lieutenant have to say if Paddy were to opt for the bunkhouse? The Scotsman saw his dilemma and shook his head when the boy turned from the bunkhouse. Paddy remembered that even if the old man's connection with sheep were to be discovered, he was supposed to know nothing about it. He took his gear into the warmth.

"Well hello, Paddy. How's Poplar Fork?"

"'Tis the only place to be if you're for silence and snow,"

the boy said glumly. Not only could he not make up his mind about the villainy of these men, it also now seemed that the lieutenant and the Scotsman both took it for granted that he was going to spy on them.

"Where's your dog?"

Jesus, Mary, and Joseph! Once the Bar L men saw how closely Dorrga stuck to the old Scotsman it wouldn't take them all that long to smell a rat. Or a sheep. Paddy struggled for a casual attitude. "Likes soldier food, I guess." He unrolled his blankets and shed reeking clothes for the first time since he had left here, spending the remainder of the day bathing and washing clothes, which he festooned on lariats strung every which way in the near-empty bunkhouse.

He recognized the grizzled puncher, who had offered to quit with him the night old Lawson burst in with rifle and lantern. "Would ye be knowin' where Jug and Ottie might be?" he asked.

The older man scratched his head. "Be in this evening, I guess. They come down from the line cabin last week just after the news."

"What news?"

The grizzled rider gave Paddy an odd look. "Same news as brought you. Them sodbusters in Ruby heerd it and the whole danged town got the scours." He grinned. "Yessiree, boy, us Bar L ruffians's welcome as the flowers in May these days—long as them savages run loose."

Paddy was thoughtful. How had the news gotten here ahead of him? He put on his mackinaw and went out to the smithy.

The farrier didn't know how the news had reached the Bar L either—only that suddenly one day everyone had known. "But I don't see a soul frettin'," Paddy protested. "Is no one fears Indians here?"

The farrier laughed. "Ain't no Indians in this country, boy. Ain't been none for years. You want to know who started it, I think it was old Bill hisself. Just his little way of lettin' them sodbusters know they still can't make it in this country unless they stay on the good side of the Bar L."

"What was the soldiers chasin' over the mountain then?"

"You tell me. Most o' the time they're chasin' their own shadows."

Paddy shrugged. No use trying to tell anything new to a man who already knows all he wants to know. He slipped back into the mackinaw as he left the smithy fire, jamming ungloved hands deep in the pockets as he crossed the open space back to the bunkhouse. His hand went through the bottomless pocket. Would he ever remember to sew the motherless thing up?

Though the lieutenant had dredged up some obscure regulation to keep his men out of the warm and nearly empty bunkhouse, he had sensed at the last moment just how little more randygazoo his long-suffering troop was disposed to accept. It had been settled that until he could confer with Lawson and be on his way again, the troop would accept potluck in the Bar L cookhouse. There would never have been room to seat them all at once if all the Bar L riders had been here, but most of them were off in Ruby with the old man, apparently to make sure the peerless sodbusters would not be murdered in their beds. Supper, Paddy decided, would have proceeded more smoothly if they could all have managed to stay in town another half hour. As it was, the rest of the Bar L burst in cold and hungry just in time to watch the last drops of gravy go down strange gullets.

"What the hell you doin' *here?*" Lawson roared. "Why ain't you out chasin' Indians?" In spite of his roaring, Paddy gained the impression that the old wild man was secretly pleased. He glanced around for the Scotsman but he was nowhere in sight. Now how had the old sheepman managed that?

As Lawson rounded on Paddy, the boy had a feeling of *déjà vu.* Surely he had played out this scene once already in the bunkhouse. "What're *you* doin' here?" the old man snarled. "Why ain't you back up there on your land?"

"'Tis a cabin ye told me to build, and not to sit at me ease all winter when there's harses t' be cared for down here."

"And I suppose it's finished already?"

"The cabin, the groceries, and me patience! Ye could have warned me there'd be Indians. Ye could have given me a rifle."

Lawson's head swiveled like a bull trying to decide which way to charge. "Why didn't you take one? Take enough stores. Can't you see it ain't snowin'? Next summer's gonna be drier than the Temperance Union. Git back up there and fall timber across that stream. Take a team and a fresno and pile up dirt the second it thaws. Git enough tanks built for the whole damn herd 'cause down here on the flats there won't be a blade of grass—as all the good citizens of Ruby are gonna find out."

"And hay?" Paddy demanded. "The stack's finished at Jug and Ottie's. Reason I was comin' back was the harses. Near starved the poor beasts was."

The mad glint left Lawson's eye. "Yes," he said quietly. "See me in the morning and we'll work something out." He stumped out of the cookhouse. Hastily, the Army cook detailed men to help swamp out and, in co-operation with the Bar L cook, they got together something hot for the famished men who had just ridden in.

Paddy departed before somebody became concerned over how idleness and no dishwashing might tend to corrupt the morals of the young. He lay atop his bed in the warm bunkhouse trying to sort any tiny grain of truth from all the chaff and bluster Lawson had scattered. Was the old man really crazy? Was a fox?

Paddy struggled to recall if the old man had given any of these wood-cutting and dam-building instructions the first time. He was sure Lawson had not. Old bastard had seemed in such a hurry to be rid of him that he had sent him off on an expedition he was sure would end in failure! Suddenly he knew old Lawson had either forgotten or never known about the pile of logs ready notched and peeled. *The spal-*

peen sent me out there to die and here I am like a bad penny. Now how bad, Paddy wondered, could a penny be?

Was it possible to pack in enough forage for animals to survive up there? Paddy didn't think so. Spend a summer cutting hay and it would be different. But even Jug and Ottie had come in when their small stock of hay played out. Poplar Fork was miles farther and a thousand feet higher.

How much snowfall was normal in this country? He resolved to ask some of the men in the bunkhouse if this year was abnormally dry. But he fell asleep on top of his blankets, thanks to the unaccustomed stove, and did not awaken till everyone else was snoring. He stuffed another chunk of wood in the stove and went back to bed. When he got up next morning it was snowing.

Chapter 19

By noon troopers were brushing a foot of snow off their sagging tents. It piled on the manes of horses, concealed frozen brown filth in the corral, turned the Bar L into a fairyland of glistening alabaster that elicited some creative cursing from soldiers and Bar L riders.

Paddy thanked the saints he had done his laundry yesterday, for now the bunkhouse was overflowing and the lariat clotheslines had come down. He got his gear together and spent the morning soaping his saddle and bridle. He cleaned and oiled the Peacemaker, snapped its single action on empty cylinders, and did everything one dares with a pistol in a crowded bunkhouse.

What now? Bar L men still seemed to have no inkling of the true situation. He wondered if anyone really believed the soldiers were not on a wild-goose chase. Paddy began to have his own doubts. All he had seen was old Lumpjaw and a boy. But nobody could make up so monstrous a story. There must have been a massacre. And somewhere in this snow-covered country roamed a band of angry Indians.

One thing for damned sure: Paddy was not going back up to Poplar Fork and be scalped. Lawson could build his own dams. He wondered if the old wild man had smelled sheep the first time they had met. Then Paddy remembered that his opening remarks had not been calculated to build any lasting friendship. Jug and Ottie had prepared the way—thought they were doing him a favor. Perhaps they had. But Paddy decided now that his original plan was still best: Get out of this bloody land—ride downstream until he found a real town, make his declaration to the constables about his gentleman and Mr. Bridgeman. And if he could get somebody to help him write a letter—even if it had to be in English—surely the priest could read it to his mother.

Then he had a second thought. His mother had other children to raise. As long as Paddy and his gentleman went unreported, his wages would be paid regularly to his mother and she would enjoy possession of the cottage. Once it became known that His Lordship had passed on to a better world—leaving an entailed estate and no lineal heirs in this one . . .

But that was in the future. Get out of here now, before he was sucked deeper into somebody else's war. Lawson and the Scots sheepman had both treated him with an absent-minded kindness while furthering their own schemes. Either man's salvation would needs draw him through the eye of a very small needle. And where was the old Scotsman hiding now to avoid a confrontation with Lawson?

Bad cess to them all! Lawson had told him to take what he needed. But how far might old Lawson's tentacles reach? If the sodbusters in Ruby were sufficiently terrified by the old scoundrel's Indian stories, even their sheriff might cooperate to hunt down a defaulting Irish boy. Break clean. Tell Lawson he was quitting; draw his wages and damn the man who tried to stop him!

He got into his mackinaw. *Damn that pocket!* He trudged through new knee-deep snow atop old crust toward the building where Lawson had first told the astonished Paddy he had been on the payroll for over a month.

The door was locked. He went around to peek through the window that would have been too high before all this snow. The office was dark and once his eyes accustomed he knew it was empty.

See me in the morning and we'll work out something. You could trust the old wild man about as far as you could throw an anvil. Then Paddy remembered it was no longer morning. He had completely forgotten Lawson's summons. Perhaps now the old man would save him the trouble of quitting. But where was Lawson? He trudged from building to shed to the smithy, where the farrier was shoeing an Army horse. "Don't know," the farrier said over his shoulder. "Try the lion's den if you're ready to get your head snapped off."

Paddy guessed he meant that fort where the not-up-to-snuff horses had been going. *Where the old ogre shot at me.* He glanced up at the leaden sky. Past midday and still snowing.

Next morning the snow was waist deep and still falling.

"Be over your head up there on Poplar Fork," a puncher laughed. "Better git yerself one of them dog sleds like the Rhooshians use."

Paddy hadn't thought of runners. He wandered about and found a huge freighting sleigh. Useless in Ireland's mild, rainy climate, but here . . . What difference did it make? He was not going back to Poplar Fork. But there was no point in proclaiming his plans to everyone. He spent the rest of the day studying harness and selecting four of the largest animals in the corral, doing his best to act disappointed when each turned out to be some rider's not-to-be-parted-with favorite mount. He nosebagged his two half-starved horses and wandered around behind the bunkhouse to think without interruption.

"Hard lines?" It was the Scotsman.

"How hard will they be when old Lawson learns you're here?"

The old man shrugged. "At least I know where I stand."

"And what would that be meanin'?"

The old man gave a wry grin. "Don't know, do ye? Think ye're owin' me somethin'. Did ye look for me that night?"

It shamed Paddy to admit that he had been too full of his own troubles.

"Don't take on so, lad. I didna' look for you either. Daylight I was twenty miles up the hill ridin' for Fort Rudge."

"What's there—save live soldiers and dead Indians?"

"A telegraph where Bill Lawson doesna' own the operator." The old man sighed. "Nae doot these men'll tell ye

Lawson was the man drove out the Indians and made't safe for cattle and Christians. Someday ye might ask old Bill, who ran sheep ten years before he came crowdin' in—and never once harmed an Indian. In those days there was room for a'."

Paddy stared. Was truth so precious in this country that it must always be given out in such tiny driblets? Then belatedly, he began to see the opposite side of the coin. Lawson had never gotten on with the savages. If the Scotsman had . . .

"No, lad. 'Twas no' me sold arms to the puir creatures. If 'twere, would I give them bad ammunition?"

"Lawson?"

"Killed me sheep. 'Twould be easy for me to say he did. Wrenched me heart to leave those few puir creatures to the wolves, but it was worth me life." The old man shrugged. "It may be that someday God will tell us what He knows. But no matter what I suspect, I know less than He does. Maybe even less than Lawson." And on that decisive note the Scotsman left Paddy to make up his own mind. Paddy did.

He hunted out Jug and Ottie, who lounged in the bunkhouse along with everybody else, including off-duty soldiers, waiting for it to quit snowing. "Ye heard the old man tell me to take rifle and kit," he said. "Could anybody be tellin' me how to get them whin Lawson and his key are gone?"

There was some debate among the Bar L punchers, and Paddy discovered that no one raised serious objections to prying off a locked hasp as long as the boy signed for the items he took—after which the store would be spiked shut again pending the wild man's return.

Paddy had never been turned loose in a candy store but the feeling as he entered this unheated room was analogous. There were a shotgun and three rifles in stock. Jug displayed a hitherto hidden talent as he opened the wish book to read,

"No. 7S419 This Belgian combined shotgun and rifle has a 38-55 caliber rifle barrel and a 12-gauge shotgun barrel,

side by side, as shown in the illustration. It has a snap top, the barrels are laminated finish, complete with back action locks, rebounding hammers, extension rib and pistol grip. The circular hammers—"

But he had already decided a combination of rifle and shotgun would probably share the worst points of both and few advantages. Besides, the *"Cut down musket for $2.75"* was only one sixth the price of the elegant Belgian arm, and it was much closer to the Tower musket the old Scotsman had taught him to shoot.

Jug and Ottie were unanimous in their disapproval. "Single-shot, slow to load, and it'll kick your back out of joint. You need a repeater."

There being only one other arm in the limited Bar L store, the boy ended up with an *"old Reliable sporting rifle Winchester model 1873, 44-caliber, Octagon barrel, 24" center fire, 15 shot, eight and three quarters pounds, $12.50."* He wondered if the Indians also had this load-on-Sunday-shoot-all-week weapon.

He selected ammunition and the best kit he could afford without running past his accumulated wages, which exercised the combined talents of Ottie, Jug, and a handful of beans. Finally the spending spree was over. He left most of his purchases in the bunkhouse and saddled the best unclaimed horse in the corral. It was a chestnut stud of some seventeen hands, nearly as big as an Irish hunter. He bandaged its legs against the crust underneath new snow and began a slow-motion, plunging gallop through the eight miles of unbroken trail to the fort.

Dorrga appeared from nowhere and insisted on accompanying him. Paddy didn't want the dog along. With all this new powdery snow he was more swimming than walking. But the collie refused to stay, which made the boy wonder if perhaps the Scotsman had issued some instruction.

After two miles of over-his-head snow the dog was exhausted. He helped the collie up to lie crossways of the saddle. It took both hands to keep the dog aboard, so the chestnut had his head as he plunged and bounded through the snow. They stopped repeatedly to rest, retie fraying bandages about his mount's cannons, and make water, which the intense cold was squeezing from them in prodigious quantities. But at least it finally turned too cold to snow as he drew within the final half mile of the fort. Both dog and horse were turning skittish. Did Dorrga remember the last time he had been shot at here? What was the horse thinking?

Remembering his last welcome, the boy began announcing himself as loud as he could yell. The Winchester was loaded but it reposed in its new boot, overlength barrel forcing the stock high enough to bang against his thigh each time the horse plunged. He was tempted to drop the dog and carry the gun across his saddle, but even if Lawson were not half mad, such an act could only be deemed unfriendly.

If it had still been snowing there might be some doubt about his yells getting through to the fort but, though the skies were leaden, it was beginning to look as if the snow was ready to call it quits. Still holding the collie in his arms, Paddy let the ears-back chestnut plunge another quarter mile. "Lawson!" he roared, "I'm comin' in. And don't ye go shootin' at a man o' substance."

There were horse tracks all over the snow and here near the cabin the trail was broken, even rutted. But the corral was empty. Still, a thin tendril of smoke rose from the rusting stovepipe. Hard telling what the secretive old bull was up to—though Paddy was beginning to get a pretty good idea.

"Lawson!" he yelled. "'Tis Padraig Ó Súilleabháin, elector and landowner o' Poplar Fork. Will ye be openin' that door or must I wait here blatherin' all afternoon?"

Dorrga was whining and squirming. "Be still!" Paddy snapped and the dog lay quiescent but rebellious, looking up to assure him that he would regret this error in judgment. The huge chestnut was also showing much white of eye, ears back as he tiredly walked the now-broken trail.

They were within a hundred yards and still no sign. Could the old man sleep so soundly? Maybe he was ill, or worse. "Lawson!" the boy howled. "'Tis cold out here. Will ye be openin' that door?"

Dorrga was whining and squirming again. If he'd had his mind on what he was doing Paddy might have let the dog down to finish the journey on his own. But he was too busy to worry about whatever was on the collie's mind. "Will ye stop it now!" He cuffed the dog with his free hand.

"Lawson, damn yez, open up!"

Abruptly the cabin door opened a crack and he could see the old man's white hair bristling like an irate hedgehog. "Hurry!" Lawson yelled. "I can't keep this door open all day."

"Ye were willin' enough to keep one open all night," the boy snarled as he urged his horse the last few paces.

"Hurry!" Lawson snapped, and half closed the massive, probably bulletproof door.

There was a snapping sound as if someone had squibbed off a musket without enough powder. But the noise was loud enough to warn Paddy he was being shot at.

"You murderin' spalpeen!" He took a hand from the dog to drag the Winchester from the boot. "Down now," he said. But instead of jumping gracefully to the snow, Dorrga fell heavily on his side, looking up with an I-told-you-so expression. The collie's eyes were already glazing.

Chapter 20

"Will you get in here now!" Lawson roared.

Jesus, Mary, and Joseph! It was not the old wild man shooting at him. For an instant Paddy thought of the red-eyed man with whom he had disputed a bunk. But that man had not reappeared. So who was it? No wonder the old bucko wouldn't swing the door wide. Another shot whistled and as Paddy snatched bandolier and Winchester he knew what Dorrga and the chestnut had been complaining about. If he'd had his wits about him he'd have known there were other people near. But he hadn't, so now the sodbusters had finally caught him in between as they moved to put an end to old Lawson's piratical tactics. So the collie had died like any good Irish soldier, knowing he might have lived if only his commander were less arrogant or stupid.

For a fraction of a second he dithered over dragging the dog inside but Dorrga was already dead, eyes milky where a moment ago they had been clear and intelligent. The stud screamed and reared as the boy was swinging to dismount and for a panicky moment he struggled to kick free from the stirrup. Dragging rifle and bandolier, he scrambled toward the door. Before he was through the old man had him by the collar, dragging him the rest of the way. Lawson dropped him and turned to bar the door.

They studied one another in silence. "Now don't you wish you'd minded your own business?" the old man finally asked.

"I wish I'd listened to my dog. But I was comin' out with a bit o' news."

"And what might that be?" The old man's voice was acidulous.

"Looks like somebody's already come to let ye know."

Lawson turned away to circle the thick-walled cabin, peering from each loophole. He aimed a Springfield through the side opposite the door and fired a single round.

"Ye might ha' done that once to warn me."

"If you'd shown the slightest sign of turning back," Lawson assured him, "you'd have been dead a half mile out. They were waiting for you to make me open the door."

"Is it the solid citizens of Ruby come to do yez in?"

"Not unless they've taken to wearing feathers."

"Feathers?" Then he knew what the old man was saying. In spite of being caught here he felt a sudden surge of exaltation at the knowledge that finally the old scoundrel was about to get everything he so richly deserved. "But if it's feathers they're wearin', then how would they know what I was sayin'? Is it English they're speakin'?"

"Your horse was pointed in the right direction and you were making enough racket. Did you think I was going to shoot you?"

Doesn't know or doesn't remember he shot at me once already.

"Did you?"

"The thought crossed me mind."

"Now why would I do a thing like that?"

If Lawson didn't know then Paddy must be barking up the wrong tree. But while he was trying to see what path this would lead him down the old man finally absorbed the boy's opening remark. "You were bringing news? If they know what's going on down at the main spread, then what're you doing here alone? Where're all them useless goddamn soldiers?"

Paddy laughed. "Ye'll nivver cut any great figure as a liar."

The old man inspected the loopholes again before he turned to glower. "What in hell *are* you talking about?"

"Lies. Did ye nivver hear the story about the boy cried 'wolf'?"

Lawson's puzzlement was interrupted by a fusillade. The walls of the fort were so thick that it seemed to Paddy as if the thump of bullets striking sod was louder than the sound of firing. The shooting went on at such a rate that he was not eager to put his eye to a loophole. "How many are there out there?" he asked.

The old man shrugged. "Twenty. Maybe thirty."

And every one with a repeating rifle.

"Who's been crying 'wolf'?" Lawson demanded.

But now the firing intensified and there was a blather of shrill screaming that made Paddy decide he'd better put the Winchester to work. He had never killed a man before. Never even tried. And those poor sods outside were only trying to get their own back for what white soldiers had done to their old, their young, their women. It was enough to sicken a man.

But they would not stop shooting. Paddy reminded himself that it was one of those poor misguided savages who had shot at him—killed Dorrga. Poor willing, hard-working dog. Sucked into another man's war. Paddy aimed at the broad brown face under a feather and pulled the trigger. As the face became unrecognizable he knew killing was not that hard after all. When he remembered this was the first time he had ever fired the Winchester the boy felt a small swell of accomplishment.

Lawson was firing slowly but steadily through the opposite wall. Paddy got off another shot and missed. But abruptly the half-dozen figures burrowing through the snow were moving away from him. He moved to a side wall. "What about fire?" he called over the deafening echoes of shooting in this tiny cabin.

"What about it?" Lawson continued his slow, careful shooting.

"Don't Indians shoot fire arrows or somesuch?"

The old man gave a sour laugh. "This is America, boy. Sod

don't burn here like it does in the Old Country. Not even if it wasn't under all this snow."

Now why hadn't he thought of that himself?

"Who's been crying 'wolf'?" Lawson persisted.

"You."

"They must make a different kind of brain in Ireland," the old man growled as he stepped from the loophole to reload. "You hitting anything or just wasting cartridges?"

"Killed one and maimed some. And did ye think yer own Bar L men would be believin' all that blarney about Indians ye've been makin' up to scare the poor louts as would put a plow to this country?"

"Making up?" Lawson was incredulous. "They're here, ain't they?"

"I do believe they are." Paddy fumbled another fifteen rounds into his Winchester and dedicated himself to the loophole until shooting diminished on that side of the soddy. "But when they did come there was nobody more surprised than you now, was there?"

"Oh I was surprised, all right. But I can't see why I should have been. After all, boy, turncoats are nothing new."

Paddy aimed carefully at the barely visible patch of a blanket out there. He fired and the blanket gave a convulsive leap. "Turncoats?"

"First men in these mountains. Never saw another white man for a year at a time. Lot of them took Indian wives."

"Better Indian than English."

"You really believe that, boy? If you do, you'd better join your blood brothers out there."

Paddy had thought about it but this did not seem an opportune moment. "Anyway, what's wrong with an Indian wife?"

"Nothing, boy, long as you're ready to kill your brother-in-law. Men forget who they are, where they come from. Who you suppose gave out the guns and sent those savages this way?"

Paddy started to tell him who had done it and suddenly

stopped. Jesus, Mary, and Joseph! The night the shooting started the old Scotsman had not hesitated to abandon him on the mountain. So that was why he was in such a hurry to get to Fort Rudge. All the Indians were there. Old friends, in-laws, comrades from better days.

And hadn't the old shepherd tried to warn him all along? *Y'owe me nothin'. 'Tis a cruel world, lad. If ye dinna' learn that ye're no' long for it.* The Scotsman had done everything but spell it out to him.

It was not that people were sparing with the truth in this country. It was just that their speech was not like his own. In Ireland people gave vague hints as to the direction of thought and by some intuitive process one filled in the missing spaces. How was he to know these odd Americans often meant—exactly and literally—just what they said? It was enough to make a man ponder.

But why hadn't he worked it out before now? If the country were not big enough for sheep, cattle, and plows, it would be advantageous for any one faction to wipe out the other two. What deviltry had the old Scotsman been up to that would provoke that attack on the sheep camp? Was he willing to see cattle, sodbusters, in-laws all driven from the country just so he could run more of the same woolly beasts that had driven his people from their crofts in Roscommon?

New land. Freedom and justice for all. The only consolation Paddy had was that he had not volunteered to come here. His gentleman had brought him and see what Himself got for his troubles. If he didn't start shooting better, Paddy was sure to get the same.

He squinted through the loophole, ducked back, and blinked dusty tears as a bullet gouged sod from the edge of it. It dropped to the mudsill floor between his feet. He picked it up. Not even misshapen. It had rifling marks and a faint coppery tinge; seemed about as heavy as the .44-caliber load from his Winchester.

"Getting old," Lawson said.

"Is it missin' ye are?"

The old man fired again and a shriek of uninhibited savage anguish outside answered Paddy's question. Old Lawson might use glasses to read but he was shooting well enough.

"Not one single living relative."

"Sounds like me gentleman. And him leavin' th'estate entailed."

"What's that?"

"Means the Queen—and bad cess to her—won't let yez cut it up. Whole shebang has to go to the eldest son. Only His Lordship would nivver call his what he sired on another man's wife."

Lawson's chuckle was like a rusty gate hinge. "Same in this country," he said. "Bar L's big enough to take care of its people. Cut it up and every one of those damned sodbusters'll starve out in a year. I'll have it back soon enough. But after they plow, how many years will it take to grow good grass again?"

Paddy peeped from a loophole and this time nobody shot at him. But suddenly the boy realized it was turning uncommon quiet outside. He wondered if these Indians were up to any dirty Irish tricks. It was time for the boy to remember where he came from. "Would ye be havin' another gun around here? Somethin' old ye'd not mind losin'?"

Lawson pointed to the jumble of saddlery and other odds and ends behind the door.

"But that's a good gun!" Paddy protested as he handled the high-hammered double-barreled shotgun.

"Won't be worth a damn to us when we're dead."

Paddy conceded the point. He began punching up the fire. Meanwhile, taking care not to stick too much barrel out the hole, he aimed at the half-dozen broad brown faces that were . . . What on earth were they up to out there?

He squinted. The sun was not out but there was a brief dying burst of illumination in the western sky. After a moment, through watering eyes, he saw what the Indians were doing. They were rolling giant snowballs. Behind each yard-wide, slowly moving ball, an Indian was working his shielded way toward the fort.

He rubbed his eyes and waited for them to stop watering. Then he aimed at the edge of the nearest snowball, trying to hold a bead on the place where from time to time a buckskin-gloved hand would appear. It appeared again and in his excitement Paddy jerked the trigger. But the loaded rifle was so heavy that his bullet had shattered that hand before his twitch could spoil his aim. He pumped another round in and lined up on the next snowball, waiting for another hand.

But the Indians learned that lesson promptly and no more hands were offered for trituration. He squinted at the snowballs, trying to guess how much resistance a yard of packed snow would offer. How high did the ball lay on fresh, powdery snow? He aimed at its bottom edge and fired. There was a commotion behind the snowball that reminded him of the antics of decapitated chickens. He had gotten his Indian the long way through.

"You wasting more cartridges, boy?"

"Take a look for yourself! I've got to reload."

Lawson crossed to Paddy's loophole and put two quick rounds into two snowballs. The Indians decided it was not so good an idea as it had seemed in the planning stages.

Paddy finished reloading and checked the stove. He tried to remember which wall. Finally he decided it was the side to the right of the door where he had first had that intuition. He put finger to lips and motioned Lawson out of the way. When the old bucko stood aside Paddy thrust the double-barreled shotgun far out through the loophole.

Immediately hands tried to wrestle it away from him. Immediately afterward there was an anguished howl as hands struggled to let go. Paddy pulled the gun back in, wrinkling his nose at the smell of burning flesh. The skin of somebody's palms still sizzled around red-hot metal.

"Where'd you pick that up?" Lawson asked.

"It's an Irish trick. But you must always remember that, though we sometimes kill one another, 'tis always done in a spirit of true Christian love."

Chapter 21

With nightfall and an even more intense cold outside the Indians seemed to lose their enthusiasm. "How many were there out there?" Paddy had asked this before and couldn't remember the answer.

Lawson hung coats and feed sacks over the loopholes, then struck a seven-day stink. While it sizzled and sputtered he looked for a candle, which he found just as the sulfur match finally burst into a reluctant flame. "Maybe thirty."

Paddy wrinkled his nose at the hell-fire smell. "Wonder what happened to me horse."

Lawson shrugged and shawled a blanket over his shoulders. "Depends on whether they've a taste for dog today." Then as he saw the pain in Paddy the old man relented. "Sorry, boy."

There was a long silence and then he growled, seemingly to himself, "Man shouldn't ever have just one dog or one horse. Ought to have forty or fifty of them and then when one dies it doesn't take it all out of you at once."

Paddy struggled to contain his outrage. This lying old hypocrite going sentimental! "Did ye ivver love anything was not a part of yourself?"

Glacial eyes focused on the boy. "If ever you live to my age, you'll wake up nights to remember what you asked me."

"Well did you?"

When Lawson rounded on him Paddy was reminded that there remained still some of the old bucko in this wild man. "I had a wife and I had a son!" he snarled. "One died and one hung herself."

And now did yez ivver put yer foot in it! But before he could begin apologies the old man was talking again. Only this time the old man was not shouting. "You're young, boy. Think the world's come to an end because your dog died. It's time you learned life's got worse in store for you." Those terrible eyes burned into Paddy for a moment and then the old man was mumbling to himself. "Goddamn sodbusters bringing families in here!" He looked up again. "Think twice before you ever talk your sweetheart into settling this country, boy. It's no place for women."

Nor much of a place for Irishmen. That accursed seven-day match had stunk up the cabin until he could scarcely breathe. Then he saw what was really happening. Somebody had plugged the stovepipe. Smoke was squirting from every crack and fissure in the sheet-iron stove.

He looked up and even by candlelight the movement on the snow-laden sod roof was visible. Paddy was pointing his rifle skyward when the old man stopped him. "Sod's too thick," he said in a low voice. "Now watch, boy, and I'll show *you* a trick."

For an Indian to have gotten up there without collapsing the snow-burdened sod roof was a minor miracle. Paddy wondered how much more weight it would support before the whole roof came tumbling down upon them. It even occurred to him to wonder how much knowledge of houses these simple savages possessed. Was there some Stone Age genius out there who had with one giant intellectual leap divined the possibilities of blocking the chimney in a tight house? Or was that just an afterthought to weighting down the roof until it fell in?

Lawson took the stewpot off the stove. He hastily lifted a stove lid, tossed something in, and slammed the lid back down over gushing smoke. He motioned Paddy to a corner far from the stove and down where the air was still clear. There was a soul-shattering whump-bang as the shotgun shell went off, lifting every stove lid momentarily and jetting more smoke into the room. But more importantly, the explosion lifted a plug of snow from the pipe. There was a howl from the roof, and sod sifted as somebody danced. Paddy wondered if it was fright or if somebody looking down the stovepipe had just traded eyelashes for ashes.

Smoke and soot smuts filled the room, making breathing impossible unless he kept his nose to the dirt floor. He lay gasping, heard movement, and saw with sudden horror that the mad old man was putting more wood in the stove. But moments later the fire blazed and drew fresh air through each loosely blinded loophole.

Lawson put the pot back on the stove and dished up stew. Each retired to his corner, as far as possible from the loopholes, and ate hurriedly. The moment they had scoffed down the stew the old man pinched out the candle. They uncovered loopholes and approached them with the circumspection of men who would prefer not to have a sharp stick in the eye.

But there were no surprises. "They never was much for night fights," Lawson rumbled.

"Would they be givin' up and goin' away?"

"I wouldn't go stickin' my head out to see. They'll camp just out of sight somewhere with maybe just one man watching."

"I could do with some sleep meself."

"They won't. Instead of resting like sensible men they'll sing and howl all night cooking up a new batch of medicine."

Paddy was weighing the possibilities of escape when the old man reminded him, "They got all the horses."

Had they? Paddy remembered how his chestnut had screamed and reared and dumped him on this fort's doorstep. Was the stallion mortally wounded or just scared? If it turned up down at the Bar L with his saddle, would anyone be curious or compassionate enough to come looking for him?

The Army was supposed to be looking for Indians. He squinted into the slightly less impenetrable darkness outside the loophole, trying to make out some outline against the starlit snow. Where was the full moon now that he needed it?

No matter how he squinted the boy could see nothing. Had they piled up something out there to blind the loophole? He thought about heating the shotgun barrel again but they probably wouldn't bite twice on the same bait. He thrust the cold gun barrel out through the loophole and waved it around. He could feel no obstruction.

Then he had another idea. He left the gun barrel sticking out of the loophole.

Suddenly he was shivering. But he knew the size of the woodbox as well as the old man. He let go of the shotgun and slipped into his mackinaw. He kilted a blanket around his waist. When he pulled the chilled shotgun back in he didn't need a light to confirm his suspicions. He could feel the dusting of new-falling snow on top of the double barrels.

"Worse for them outside," the old man said. "And leastways my eyes ain't goin' so bad as I was thinking there for a spell."

Paddy was reassured to discover that he was not the only one afflicted with doubts and fears of this nature. He sighed. How must it have been when the old man was young to live day after day, year after year with this constant tension, the knowledge that at any moment Indians might decide to raid? Small wonder that Lawson's woman hung herself. The real wonder was that the old man had lived a lifetime with the memory and not gone dottier than he was.

"Try to sleep, boy. You'll need your wits about you come daylight."

"Wake me," Paddy offered, "and I'll stand a watch for yez."

"I'll do that."

But when Paddy woke the next time he saw that the old man had stood his own watch all night and a barely perceptible gray now leaked through the loopholes.

"Old men don't sleep all that much," Lawson explained.

But Paddy suspected what he meant was, old men don't trust boys not to fall asleep. Lawson had already punched up the fire and put coffee to boil. Paddy yawned and stretched, then put an eye to the loophole. "Jesus, Mary, and Joseph, what's that?"

Lawson pushed him aside to peer at the line of Indians. They were not crouching now. They stood in full view, rifles in hand, as they walked parade-ground erect and shoulder to shoulder across the cruel, coverless snow toward the cabin.

"Is it an army they have?" Paddy demanded. "I nivver knew Indians wore uniforms."

"Better load your rifle," Lawson said. "And say a prayer over your bullets."

"Prayer?"

"Those'll have to be the magic shirts."

To Paddy they looked like cheap imitations of the blouses the cavalry troop wore, save that these shirts were now bedecked with bits of feather and bone, shards of mirror sewn into beadwork. "Magic shirts?"

"Supposed to stop bullets."

He remembered the Scotsman's explanation of what had convinced the Indians they dared attack Fort Rudge. "Now where'd you ever hear about them shirts?"

"What you trying to prove, boy? You think soldiers can keep a secret?"

"If I was a soldier I'd not be puffed up over what I did."

"I don't see you waving no white flags here."

"I didn't start this." Paddy put his eye to the loophole again. "But won't they know the magic's done with?"

"Maybe. And maybe they've been all night long singing some new medicine into that flannel." Lawson aimed his Springfield at the wizened man at the end of the line. One down, twenty to go. He emptied his rifle and still they came. Paddy took his place at the single loophole on that side of the cabin. Was he too nervous to hit anything at this range?

Then he saw that he was hitting them. They kept right on

coming. By the time his rifle was empty the Indians were too close for him to be able to aim at the extremes of the line. Lawson took his place.

"Goddamn it!" the old man snarled, and wiped blood from his ear. Suddenly Paddy saw it had not come from in front. Somebody had stuck a rifle through the loophole in the opposite wall and was shooting into the cabin. He almost grabbed the barrel before he realized the Indians might have adopted his Irish tricks. He snatched boiling, long-forgotten coffee from the stove and flung it. An instant later he cautiously dragged the rifle in the rest of the way by the wooden part beneath the barrel. It was the same kind of Winchester he had been shooting: a load-on-Sunday-shoot-all-week gun. The rear sight was sprung into its highest, shoot-harder notch.

He turned the rifle around and began firing back out the loophole. The captured rifle hardly kicked, and there was less noise than from his own. He ejected a cartridge without firing and dropped it in his pocket before reloading his own Winchester.

Old Man Lawson was skipping nimbly from one loophole to the next, pouring a steady fire into the Indians, who still seemed to believe in their magic shirts despite firsthand evidence to the contrary all around them. There couldn't be half of the original line left. Were they getting reinforcements from somewhere?

Paddy fired again and missed. He missed three times before he finally forced a .44-caliber slug through the aura of a magic shirt. Hackles rose as he considered the possibility that there might be some real magic to these prosaic garments. But if there was, Lawson's slow and deadly shooting seemed to have counteracted it. Paddy was reloading again when he saw that the Indians had finally dropped to the snow again and were retreating just like men who know perfectly well that bullets can kill, and have already killed too many.

Lawson began making fresh coffee. Paddy reloaded both

Winchesters. He lowered the sight on the captured weapon, checked its action, and decided that in spite of rough usage by someone with no knowledge of the affinity between guns and oil, the weapon would still shoot.

But why hadn't it been shooting any better? With all those repeating rifles out there, surely they ought to have put a few rounds inside this cabin. Then he remembered the Scotsman's story about bad ammunition. He fished the ejected round from his pocket. Like the spent slug that had puffed dirt in his eyes, this bullet was copper-jacketed.

"Would ye be knowin' why anybody'd be makin' a ball out o' that?" Paddy asked.

Lawson turned from the coffee pot to squint at the cartridge Paddy handed him. He put on pince-nez and studied it. He took them off to squint at the boy and for a moment Paddy saw the same mad glint he remembered from the night in the bunkhouse. But sanity returned and the old man said, "Keeps the lead from breaking up. That way the bullet goes in deeper."

It sounded like something the English would invent.

"Did you get any this time?" Lawson asked.

"Don't know. Must've scalded the bejaysus out of one the way he let go of this."

Lawson studied the rifle with new interest. "Where'd you get yours?" he finally asked.

"Out of your store." Paddy told him how the Bar L riders had unanimously decided to pry off the lock and then spike the door shut. If the old man was annoyed he did not show it.

"How many Indians are there still out there?" the boy asked. "Will they fight to the last man or will we be gettin' out o' here before the last stick o' wood and the last o' that bucket o' water's gone?"

"You're on better terms with them than I am, boy. Why don't you ask?"

"The Indians?"

"Jesus, Mary, and Joseph."

Paddy was too wrung out for anger. Besides, if a copper jacket made the slug go in deeper, why weren't these Indian bullets doing more damage? He squinted at the lettering around the base of the cartridge. He could make out letters, but his knowledge of reading was not sufficient to tell him if it was English or some other language. "If they're shootin' the same rifle as me," he finally asked, "why do theirs smoke so much? Would we be shootin' that new smokeless powder me gentleman was always harpin' about?"

"No smokeless powder in this country that I know about," the old man said. "Chances are theirs is just old."

Paddy put a cautious eye to a loophole. Nothing. He circled the cabin checking the four holes. There was not even a dead Indian in sight.

"Lost us a chance there, boy. Could have got another couple while they were dragging them off."

How many more could there be? All the skirmishes and set pieces were blending together. It was hard to realize that yesterday evening he had never killed a man. Now he had lost count. He remembered as a lad how he had asked the old men about soldiering, if it was hard to kill one of God's creatures. He had been puzzled by their replies—even after he had gotten the same answer so many times he knew they could not all be lying about a soldier's life. "No, lad," the old men always told him. "Killin's the least part of it."

The way he felt right now Paddy was willing to wipe out the College of Cardinals for a nice cuppa tea and an hour of quiet. He was dwelling on how long it had been since last he tasted Christian cooking when he heard the shooting start again.

Chapter 22

This time there was an amazing lot of shooting. Louder than before, and it seemed to be coming from all sides. Bullets thumped into the cabin walls. Paddy remembered how one had gouged debris into his eyes yesterday. The walls of this sod-roofed fort had been half a yard thick once. How long could they stand this ceaseless pecking away with underpowered ammunition? He glanced upward. Even before the snow there had been considerable strain on those ancient pole rafters. When would the whole fort collapse?

There was something else odd about it all. These Indians were on the run from the debacle at Fort Rudge. Their ammunition was old and bad, but how could defeated, fleeing men have carried enough to keep up this ceaseless fire? He edged up to a loophole.

Yesterday these openings had been scarcely large enough to aim through. In the course of the battle they had eroded to afford a wider field of fire. And conversely, the cabin's interior was that much more exposed to incoming fire. But at this moment Paddy could not see a single source of all the shooting. "Would ye be seein' any o' thim on your side?"

"Ary hide nor hair," Lawson called back.

Was an Indian capable of anything so complex as binding a repeating rifle to a pole and firing it from cover? The fusillade dwindled but still bullets thumped dully into the sod wall. Lawson poured himself a cup of coffee. His white hair still bristled like an irate hedgehog. Blood was flaking from his nicked ear. "Will they ever run out of bullets?" Paddy asked. *Did they have some stored nearby?*

The old man shrugged and spooned sugar into coffee.

Paddy poured himself a cup and they retreated to opposite corners of the square building, as far as possible from the lines of fire. Still the shooting went on. Yesterday the boy would have supposed it was cover for a close-in assault but today the loopholes were too wide for surprises.

He wished he were as confident about his own ammunition supplies as the Indians seemed about theirs. How much longer? Half of the poor creatures out there must be dead already. But theirs were all dead. Were they like King Brian, who held his life lightly so long as he cleared the strangers from Ireland? "Would ye be havin' any more o' these Winchester cartridges?" he asked.

Lawson pointed behind the door. Paddy had been meaning to ask why, with all this space, the old man's bunk had been high in one corner, kitchen gear beneath it, and everything else heaped in a desperate tangle behind the door. It seemed as if there might have been a great many other things stored here recently. He picked through bridles and bits of saddlery and found a box of cartridges. "This all?"

"If you can't finish off ten or fifteen men with fifty rounds, you may as well pack up and go home," Lawson growled. He put his cup down and peeped cautiously out.

Paddy did likewise. There were two sticks of firewood still unburned. How comfortable were the Indians out there in the snow? If they'd left Fort Rudge with soldiers behind them, how much food could they have picked up on the way? Then he remembered Lawson's empty corral. Damn the horse-eating Indians! What was there left to eat in this cabin?

The bucket was empty but Lawson had placed it to catch the slightly muddy drip that filtered through the sod roof near the stovepipe. Once they ran out of wood that drip would freeze up again. He pawed through near-empty sacks and found oats—not oatmeal, but the same kind that went in the nosebags of horses. But oats could stave off hunger as long as there was fire to cook them. He put the bucket on the stove and poured them in. If the wood gave out before the oats boiled at least they would have soaked closer to chewability. How much longer? Had the Indians eaten his horse? Or Dorrga? He felt a sudden pang as he thought of the collie. Somebody was going to pay for that. But half of them had already paid and he didn't feel much better about it. How many men's lives did it take to equal one dog's?

Lawson sat in his corner neither approving nor disapproving the boy's preparations. Outside the fusillade had degenerated into a desultory popping, apparently only intended to keep them pinned in the cabin. "When did they come?" Paddy asked.

"About an hour before you did."

"Would they be knowin' how we're fixed for water and food and such?"

"Probably."

Paddy continued poking about, hoping more cartridges would turn up in some dusty corner of the empty room. He was about to ask how the Indians could know what was inside here when abruptly he changed his mind.

Jesus, Mary, and Joseph! Would he forever be a boy, swallowing whatever malarkey this pair of scoundrels saw fit to feed him? Between Lawson's lies and the old Scotsman's evasions they'd been shuttlecocking him until there was nothing left to believe in.

He had ridden out here that first time to cure sick horses. And the second time—after dark? He'd had his suspicions even then, until Lawson had explained it all away.

But the hoofprints leading off in the opposite direction? Those Indians had gotten ammunition and rifles from somewhere. He remembered how unhesitatingly Lawson had shot at the first thing that moved that night—the night Paddy found a feather in the snow.

They were still putting two or three rounds a minute into the cabin. He squinted through a loophole, suspicious of this lull. What were the blatherskites cooking up this time?

A feather proves nothing. He'd thrown it away. So dark he hadn't even been able to tell from what kind of bird it came. What if those broad-faced savages out there did wear feathers? So do birds. Might have fallen from any feathered friend flying over this fort.

He put the last wood in the stove and fanned enthusiastically with his hat. The bucket of oats and snow water was barely warm. *In the days of the Hunger they ate worse.* Despite the reviving fire he was suddenly cold again. He stuffed hands into mackinaw pockets. If the Indians didn't call it off soon he would never get around to sewing up that pocket.

"What're you going to do with your young life once we're out of here?" Lawson asked.

"Will we be gettin' out o' this alive?"

"I wasn't born this old."

There were times when the old wild man made sense in a purely Irish way. This was the talk Paddy understood, an elliptical utterance in which the listener was to deduce the unspoken meanings about having survived countless dangers, the calm confidence that he would survive one more. But there was still another level of meaning. "I don't know if I like the country or the people," Paddy said. "Besides, ye've forty men all longer wid yez."

"Some like sons to me. Others like brothers. And even Brutus is dead now."

"But why me?"

"They're good *boys*. If any one of them had enough sense to run the Bar L, he'd be off starting his own spread."

"And me?"

"Think I don't know what you've put into Poplar Fork? Man works that hard's not working for the Bar L. He's working for himself."

Paddy hadn't thought of it that way. In any event, his mind was on something else. Why did the old scoundrel have to turn gabby just when he was trying to think? As if it weren't hard enough for a groom to outthink a horse. Horse sense indeed! He struggled to remember what he had been thinking about. The effort showed in his freckled Irish face.

"It'll kill you."

"What is it would be killin' me?"

"Too much thinking, boy." Abruptly Lawson spun and aimed from a loophole. He fired and there was a groan outside. Not just one man. The enemy must have thought they were out of ammunition in here. Paddy looked out his loophole and saw nothing. Be damned if he'd waste a round just to show the flag. Wait till he could kill another one. *And here I was a good Christian never harmed a soul.*

What was it lurked just beyond the feathery edge of memory? Would the old wild man ever pack it up? Hadn't had a civil word for the boy since they'd met and now he had to be makin' speeches. Feather edge of memory. Proved nothing. Birds shed them all the time.

"Think you could run a place like the Bar L?"

Does he know I'm barely sixteen? Does he know I think he's crazy? "I could run the harses, but who'd run the men?"

"If you've got enough sense to run a horse, you'd have no trouble with men."

Paddy had often suspected as much but it was not a groom's duty to voice opinions of this nature. Still, he felt a swell of pride as he remembered the way they had rallied behind him that night in the bunkhouse. He might have led them all away and left the Bar L without a single hand. In the pig's eye he could! Only gradually did the enormity of the old man's proposition sink into him. Old Bill Lawson was offering to adopt him—make Paddy his heir!

Why?

Paddy didn't believe it for a minute. This was the kind of talk that flowed with the whiskey when old men got together. Nobody was expected to take it seriously. And yet he had learned to his dismay that in this country men often meant exactly what they said. And whiskey? If there was a drop of poteen in this cabin Paddy would have warmed himself long ago. He thrust hands deeper into his mackinaw pockets.

High-pitched Indian voices outside and then simultaneously sizzling, stinking balls were thrust through all four loopholes. Paddy steeled himself, waiting for the grenades to explode. Lawson calmly speared each with the poker and thrust it in the stove. He opened drafts and damper and within a minute the stove was roaring cheerfully, oats beginning to steam. He thrust the poker in the firebox until it burned clean, then used it to stir them.

"Now what was that?"

"Magic." The old man shrugged. "Wouldn't be surprised if it was a couple of those shirts with some herbs and gunpowder thrown in."

Paddy wondered if this was a final try or if the Indians still had something else up their sleeves. Did he have anything up his? Which of these archetypal liars was he to believe? The Scotsman had offered him the sheep. Lawson was giving him the Bar L. The luck of the Irish? Any Irishman knows fairy gold always turns out dearer than the kind men sweat and kill for. But it would be nice to have a pocketful.

A pocketful. That night he had ridden back here in the dark to see what Lawson was up to. He hadn't found just a feather. He had picked up something else—something he had stuffed into a pocket and forgotten.

He'd been going to inspect it once he got to lamplight and then this old wild man had burst into the bunkhouse and it had gotten clean out of his mind. Piece of pasteboard . . . and where had it gotten to?

Paper—pasteboard—not that plentiful in a country where men whittled shavings and saved punky wood to kindle fires. He hadn't started any fires with pasteboard. Must have slipped from his pocket or dissolved when he washed clothes—hadn't washed his mackinaw—not that heavy coat with the bottomless pocket! He dug deep and found—nothing.

Somewhere outside the shooting increased but it was farther away. Let them waste their worthless, underpowered ammunition. He took off the mackinaw and began forcing his hand deeper through that pocket, searching systematically around the skirt of the heavy garment. And in the back, mashed flat from sitting, he found a frayed and nearly worn-out piece of pasteboard.

He couldn't read it. Didn't even seem to be in English. But there was a picture of a bullet on the carton. He tossed it to Lawson.

If he had expected the old man to crumble and cringe from the weight of evidence, Paddy was disappointed. Lawson gave it an incurious glance. "Where'd you find it?"

"Outside. Could you be tellin' me what it is?"

"Looks like it was a box of .44s."

"'Tis not the same color's the stuff I'm shootin'."

"Nope. Looks like some of that funny Belgian stuff. They loaded it for African troops. Jungle fighting where you can't see fifty feet and don't want to kill your own people." The old man grinned. "If that's what our friends out there're shooting, no wonder we're still alive."

"And ye wouldn't be knowin' who was givin' it to the poor savages?"

"'Tween sheep and Indians I guess he'd stop at nothing."

Paddy sighed. "You may be right. But why would the Scotsman be storin' his no-good bullets on Bar L land?"

Lawson's eyes narrowed. "What the hell you getting at, boy?"

"'Twas not yesterday I found this. I picked it up the night you shot at me—the night the pack train left to deliver all thim guns and bullets to the Indians. Thim savages out there know who gave them bad bullets. 'Tis why they're givin' them back to you."

From the sudden glint in those old mad eyes, Paddy knew he had finally worked it out the way it must have happened. Lawson started to speak and then suddenly the shooting was louder, all around them. Lead poured into the sod walls, threatening to bring the roof down. Paddy scooted to a corner and braced himself.

Chapter 23

Then it dawned on him that this was not the weak-loaded, overage ammunition the Indians had been popping off. The noise was deafening. And gradually he realized that very little of it was hitting the fort. There were shouts. Then he heard the bugle.

His Winchester was near empty. He pulled wearily from the loophole and, with a movement that was already becoming automatic, began stuffing cartridges into the seemingly bottomless, fifteen-shot magazine. Poor damned Indians— blameless as the Irish, and he had been killing them. Now that fire-eating lieutenant would finish them off.

He was so tired, so heartsick that he was not even shocked when he realized the rifle in his lap was still cocked, probably a round in the chamber, and it was wavering in Lawson's general direction. He was reaching to let it off cock before the old assassin could give him what-for when he glanced up and knew the old man had already seen his carelessness.

Then he understood that it had not been his only carelessness. Lawson's Springfield pointed straight at Paddy. "I told you thinking would kill you," the old man said.

So that was the way it was to be. Now that the cavalry had finally come looking for him—he wondered if the chestnut had come home without a rider or if it had been the farrier kept nagging away until the lieutenant had ridden out of the warmth of camp. What difference did it make? Lawson was going to kill him and lay it on the Indians. With all this shooting who would ever know?

As he stared into the muzzle of the Springfield, saw that

hedgehog shock of white hair and that terrible blue eye glaring across a sight, Paddy knew it was too late for Confession. Too late for an Act of Contrition. Too late to be sorry he hadn't believed the Scotsman instead of this double-dealing snake in the grass. Too late for everything except one possible—only chance.

"Ye're makin' a mistake," he said. Without waiting for an answer he pulled the trigger, praying there would be a cartridge in the chamber of the half-loaded rifle.

Two rifles went off at once. Until now they had been firing outside through the loopholes. Now twin explosions reverberated in this square cabin until he knew he would never hear again. Would Lawson?

While Paddy stared, nearly losing his grip on the Winchester, he saw the sudden look of blank surprise as a third eye appeared just below the white bristles that no longer resembled a demented hedgehog. Now he was just a poor crazy old man and Paddy had killed him. He remembered the look of blank surprise the day they had broken the stallion of scraping riders off under low-lying branches. Neither of them would ever do it again.

"You're lucky to be alive," the lieutenant said once all the shooting and shouting and are-you-all-right-in-there were over.

Paddy wondered. Most of the Bar L punchers had ridden out with the soldiers once the chestnut came home with a bullet nick across his rump. Now they were riding back to the main spread, and the boy noted absently how much easier these eight miles were now that forty horses had pounded the snow down. Lawson was coming back too, crossways of an Army horse, wrapped in an Army tarp. He made a surprisingly small bundle.

And not a soul among them even suspected Paddy. Dimly, the boy began to understand that, no matter how much of a scoundrel the mad old bull of Bar L had been, his secrets must die with him—unless Paddy was also willing to die.

Once somebody got around to asking he would claim ignorance. "I turned around for more bullets and there was Himself already dead." In time maybe even Paddy would come to believe it happened that way.

He was terribly afraid he was going to weep in front of all these men. But the puzzling part was that now he wasn't thinking of all the poor blameless Indians he had killed. He thought only of old Lawson, who had known exactly what he was doing—had struggled until the final moment to throw dust in Paddy's eyes. Had Satan ever offered a full-found estate with men and cattle during those forty days in the wilderness?

But I was never tempted.

What would they offer him now? He was of no more use to the Scotsman. Lawson was all through making offers. The ride had ended somehow without him being aware of it and now they were all back at the Bar L, and in spite of old Lawson's death, it had turned into some kind of a celebration as Bar L riders and cavalrymen congratulated one another on putting an end to all them treacherous Indians and what was Paddy doing out here away from the cookhouse, away from the bunkhouse, all alone leaning on the top pole of the corral staring at horses who seemed to understand what troubled him much better than those shallow louts whooping it up back in there—and bad cess to them all!

"I can lay the whole world at your feet."

As he heard those silken words Paddy's hackles rose with the knowledge that what they had told him as a child was all true. No matter how the English and the Protestants and all the smart and smooth-talking ones might laugh, Evil walks in the world and the Prince of Lies stood behind him in the gloaming. But when he spun it was only the old Scotsman. "But I'll offer you nothing," the old man said dryly, "save the knowledge that it wasna' your bullet."

"My what? What is it you'd be sayin'?"

"Ye fooled the others, lad. But 'tis no' the first time ye've fought for your life, so why would ye be sleepwalkin' if't weren't somethin' bad happened in that cabin?"

Paddy wondered if he would be that transparent to the others. "He tried to make me think 'twas you armed the Indians."

"Aye. He'd do that. And then used you to fight them off till the soldiers came and ye were no longer needed."

"How did you guess?"

"Lawson had a way of not needin' people after a while."

Paddy supposed he should have guessed it. "Yez were friends once?"

"In a way of speakin'."

There was a long silence. "Poor man losin' a wife and child that way," Paddy said. "'Tis small wonder—"

"Oh aye," the Scotsman said. "Lost 'em a' right. 'Tis a pity he didna' tell ye that before they were his, the bairn was mine."

"Yours?"

"And the wife. More's the fool I was, but then I was near as young as you are now. When he tired of a woman with another man's bairn I was too stiff-necked to have them back."

Another long silence and then Paddy was back picking at it, unable to let it be. "But how'd you know I—"

"A body still warm, and a' the powdermarks?"

"I'd best tell them all—"

"Don't. The bullet that barely made it through the top o' that twisted brain had a copper jacket. You and Lawson were pumpin' pure lead."

Jesus, Mary, and Joseph! I wasn't aimin' and 'twas no miracle. A stray bullet from outside. Maybe 'twas a miracle.

"So what'll ye be doin' now, lad? Be bringin' over your sweetheart?"

"'Tis no country for women."

"Ye'd believe that!" The old man sighed. "The old order changeth," he quoted. "Another year and the rails'll be to

Ruby. By the time ye've scraped up passage your lass'll be comin' in style on the steam cars."

"But I'm not heir to the Bar L now."

"Of course y'are."

"With Himself dead and not a word in writin'?"

"Are ye no' the owner of a section up at Poplar Fork?" While Paddy struggled to remember this the old man added, "There is no Bar L. 'Twas a' in old Lawson's mind, like a snake chopped to bits and still doesn' ken it's dead."

Paddy had arrived in late October and never known warm weather in America. "Is it true there are such things as snakes?" he asked.

"Ye'll find out come summer. And so would have Lawson if he'd lived t' see these cowboys settle down to the knowledge that each and every one of them is a landowner—and a good catch for some sodbuster's daughter." The old man studied Paddy with amusement. "'Tis a landowner and a bachelor y'are. Best ye be prepared for some changes."

"Too many changes I've seen," Paddy grumped. "And since everyone wants t' know me plans, what's yours?"

"I'd thought of Roscommon."

Paddy tried to think of himself once more adjusting to the limited horizons of County Down. And the old man had been here three times longer than Paddy had lived. "Ye'll be back in a fortnight," he predicted.

"I know. 'Tis somethin' this country does t' ye. Is there somethin' I could bring ye from the Old Country?"

"Me mother, me sister, and three brothers," the boy said promptly. "And see that she's collected me wages from whoever's His Lordship now."

The old man boggled for a moment, then came close to smiling. He spent some time extracting directions to an estate on the east shore of Lough Neagh, seven miles west of the Lord Mayor's of Belfast, and a half hour's canter down from Antrim. "Ye can't miss it," Paddy assured him. The Scotsman assured him that he would not and disappeared, leaving the boy to poke suspiciously at all these neat knots to the package of his life.

Life had never been this good—even at home. Since he had landed in this godforsaken country he'd known nothing but unmitigated disaster. Could his mother and his brothers and sister survive in Poplar Fork?

A damn sight better here than in the ditches of County Down once the news reached home that his gentleman was no longer paying wages, that the estate was up for grabs, and devil take the cottagers. Get potatoes in this spring and they'd survive. And the back of his hand to whoever tried to get him out of Poplar Fork!

But if the old Scotsman had it right, nobody would try. Lawson had held the Bar L together. Without him . . . the sodbusters would come. The railroad would bring more. But clever old Lawson had outfoxed himself. Or maybe he had guessed it would end up this way. Cattle were finished. But as long as one Bar L rider hung onto his section, planted and watered his land and kept it from blowing away, there would be someone to remember the old bucko who chased out the Indians.

But there was still something askew. The Scotsman had tried to tell him Lawson died from a copper-jacketed, underpowdered Indian bullet. Could Paddy have missed?

He had been tired, confused, frightened. Maybe he had missed. Maybe at that moment a stray slug had come through one of those gradually widening loopholes. Maybe Jesus, Mary, and Joseph had taught Lawson not to mock them—had saved Paddy from mortal sin.

Whosoever looketh on a woman to lust after her hath committed adultery with her already in his heart. Paddy had been confessing sins of this nature for several years. The principle could, by analogy, be applied to murder. Even if he had not hit the old man, Paddy had done his honest and sincere best to send him to Hell.

Suddenly the boy knew there were more important things. Lawson had told him to take an outfit. Get back up to Poplar Fork and fix that dam. How long would it be before every puncher in that bunkhouse realized there was no longer anyone to pay him another month's wages? How long before they stripped the ranch clean to grubstake their own sections—or to ride long and hard away from this country?

Paddy had already selected all the things he would need for a winter in Poplar Fork. Even found the sleigh he would use. Quietly, while the rest of them smoked and gabbed in the warmth, he got his gear together and harnessed up. He studied the sleigh and saw room for seed oats and wheat. He snitched a sack of seed praties from the cookhouse root cellar, and one of onions. By midnight he was ten miles back up the trail.

Then, while the horses rested, he tried not to think of how dreary a winter would be up there without Dorrga. And while his horses blew and his mind wandered, Paddy finally put the final link to the chain.

He searched his pocket and found the copper-jacketed slug that had knocked dust in his eyes. What he did not find was the copper-jacketed cartridge he had pumped from the other Winchester he had pulled from an Indian's hands. He had mixed it in with a pocketful of the unjacketed lead cartridges he had been shooting all day. One round of the short-range ammunition Lawson had sold the Indians, knowing they could accomplish nothing with it, that the soldiers at Fort Rudge would finish them off. The range had been just enough to cross the cabin from Paddy's corner to old Lawson's.

He clucked the horses into a trot and began saying an Act of Contrition.